T0126617

The Baby Can Sing
AND OTHER STORIES

The Baby Can Sing
and
Other Stories

Judith Slater

Winner of the 1998
Mary McCarthy Prize in Short Fiction
Selected by Stuart Dybek

Sarabande Books
LOUISVILLE, KENTUCKY

Copyright © 1999 by Judith Slater

FIRST EDITION

All rights reserved.

No part of this book may be reproduced without written permission of the publisher. Please direct inquiries to:

Managing Editor
Sarabande Books, Inc.
2234 Dundee Road Suite 200
Louisville, KY 40205

LIBRARY OF CONGRESS CATALOGING-IN-PUBLICATION DATA

Slater, Judith, 1951-
    The baby can sing & other stories / by Judith Slater.
        p.   cm.
    "Winner of the 1998 Mary McCarthy prize in short fiction, selected by Stuart Dybek."
    ISBN 1-889330-34-5 (cloth: alk. paper). — ISBN 1-889330-35-3 (pbk.: alk. paper)
    1. United States—Social life and customs—20th century—Fiction.
I. Dybek, Stuart, 1942–   . II. Title. III. Title: Baby can sing, and other stories.
    PS3569.L262B33   1999
    813'.54—dc21   99-11464
                                                                    CIP

Cover painting: *Flying Baby: Ellie #2*, by Suzy Kitman. Oil on paper. Courtesy of the artist.

Cover and text design by Charles Casey Martin.

Manufactured in the United States of America.
This book is printed on acid-free paper.

Sarabande Books is a nonprofit literary organization.

To Gerald Shapiro

♦

and to the memory of Basil Saunders

Acknowledgments

These stories first appeared (some in different form) in the following publications: "The Baby Can Sing" in *Crab Creek Review*; "The Bride's Lover" in *Greensboro Review*; "The Glass House" in *Flyway*; "The Fat Dancer" in *Crosscurrents*; "The Things We Find" in *Colorado Review*; "Pretty Night" (under the title "A Father's Wish") in *Redbook*; "Phil's Third Eye" in *Beloit Fiction Journal*; "The Salt of the Earth" (under the title "Television Secrets") in *Frontiers*; "David Morning" in *ACM: Another Chicago Magazine*; "Sandra Dee Ate Here" in *Pangolin Papers*; "Soft Money" in *Baltimore Review*; and "Water Witch" in *Sonora Review*.

Contents

Foreword

It's part of the magic of literature that, despite the abstract nature of language, we read with our senses—those gateways to the emotions—as well as with our intellects. The medium of "words, words, words" can be made to seem almost physical, and I imagine that each reader has his own particular set of sometimes physical responses which, once triggered, serve as dependable tests for when a work of art has engaged him on a visceral level.

"Make them laugh; make them cry," Wilkie Collins advised when asked the secret to a successful nineteenth-century novel, but, though we read to be moved, the measure of emotional involvement needn't be tears or laughter. It might be instead a certain indefinable *frisson*, a hairstand, a shiver of both skin and soul when we confront the sublime at, say, the conclusion of Joyce's "The Dead," or the opening of *The Duino Elegies*.

Or, as anyone who's attended a reading (or sat around a campfire spinning tales) probably knows, the gauge might be a collective release more telling than applause—an actual exhalation as if everyone in the room has been holding their breaths.

And there are responses that aren't exactly physical but not strictly intellectual either: the Would You Buy This For A Gift test, or the Will You Read This A Second Time. For readers who are also writers there's the Do You Wish You Wrote This Yourself response.

There's a test that every editor, every writing teacher, and every contest judge inescapably becomes acquainted with: that happy realization that they've stopped reading a story critically or judgmentally and, caught up in the spell of the story, have forgotten the assignment, the contest, and their role as anything other than engaged reader.

That was my experience when I came upon Judith Slater's collection *The Baby Can Sing*. I'll admit that nowhere did it make me cry, but frankly I find laughter to be a more rare and valuable gift than tears anyway, and stories such as "The Bride's Lover," "Phil's Third Eye," and "The Salt of the Earth" had me laughing.

What's more, this collection passed a test that I think of as the Driscoll response, a factor I first became aware of several years ago when Charles Baxter and I were driving together on a Michigan highway, talking about stories—what else?—but rather than our own work, we were telling one another stories that a mutual friend, Jack Driscoll, had written. (This was a year or so before Driscoll's collection would win the AWP Prize.)

I had that same urge with Judith Slater's collection, although, since the entries in the Sarabande competition are anonymous, I had no idea who had written the stories. Nonetheless, I found myself retelling them to friends: the story about the woman who invites her old boyfriend, a photographer, to her wedding to take her wedding pictures; and the bizarre story about the woman who encounters her old shrink far away in an unexpected place; and the love triangle, if love is the accurate word, about a college student whose father has an affair with one of her professors (a story that ever so vaguely evoked a recollection of Gary Cooper in *Ten North Frederick*).

And then there were stories like "Water Witch," rendered with such delicacy that though I would have liked to retell them, retelling wasn't possible—they exist only if read as written.

Judith Slater is a writer whose work rings true to experience:

her observation of the world is keen, reported in a prose distinguished by fresh imagery and clever turns of phrase. Her style is deft, not light, the difference being that deftness is an aspect of grace. Her dialogue sounds like human voices. She has an eye for subtle details, physical and psychological, that make her characters come alive and maintain their credibility, even in those instances when the unpredictable nature of life makes their situations less than credible.

Experience illuminates Judith Slater's stories, but does not limit them. She is a writer who understands that the first allegiance of fiction is to the imagination.

—*Stuart Dybek*
July, 1998

The Baby Can Sing
AND OTHER STORIES

The Baby Can Sing

And maybe even dance. If I had a baby, that's the kind of baby I'd want. After giving her a bath in the kitchen sink, while the fog lifted over the ocean, I'd tuck a towel around her waist and teach her the fox-trot. I'd watch her tiny feet, like pink seashells, trip lightly across the kitchen counter.

The baby's got rhythm. No "Itsy-Bitsy Spider" for her. She croons "Ole Man River" and "Smoke Gets in Your Eyes" and "It Never Entered My Mind"—songs that will break your heart. She doesn't know the words yet, but she's got perfect pitch. When the baby lies against my stomach and hums "Heart Like a Wheel," her whole body vibrates like a cat purring. Even when she's not humming out loud, she's humming to herself. You can hear that purr. She's pure rhythm, pure sound, that baby.

I keep her away from elevators and Muzak, from piped-in Neil Diamond and Barry Manilow. When she gets a little older I won't have to do this; she'll learn for herself to tune out old Monkees songs, used-car jingles on the radio, bad Elvis as opposed to good

Elvis. I think she already knows to do this, but you can't be too careful. She's only a baby, after all. And there are all those bad influences lurking. It's a dangerous world. So we stay away from K-Mart and malls, from enclosed spaces in general where we might hear the wrong things. We take the stairs instead of the elevator. Always, we take the stairs.

If I had a baby, I'd move with her to the seashore. Talk about rhythm! The pull of the tides in and out. I'd leave her window cracked open at night so she would hear, even in sleep, the sound of the waves. During the day, she'd dance on the beach, kicking up sand, a tiny plump Zorba against the horizon, arms lifted in a circle above her head. I want her to learn all the best songs in the world. And for that, you have to start young.

When I was pregnant, I went to the symphony, string quartets, operas. Every chance I got. You start with the classics and then branch out, that's my feeling. If you get a good grounding in Beethoven and Bach and Mozart and Verdi before you're born, you can go anywhere with it. And this baby has. Her tastes are eclectic, her standards high. You should hear her belt out "Natural Woman." And she loves anything, anything, by Bonnie Raitt. And the Weavers! She hums "Goodnight, Irene" in her sleep, while the tide comes in. And then, the next day, when we are walking downtown, she will aim her stroller toward that fantastic banjo-playing street musician and will refuse to move on until I have tossed every one of my quarters into his hat.

The baby collects seashells. She clacks them together like castanets. When she tires of that, she holds them up to her ear and listens to the sound of the ocean. I didn't teach her to do this; she picked it up on her own. Maybe she was born knowing how. That's the kind of baby she is.

I always thought I'd be afraid to have a baby: afraid of that vulnerable soft spot on her skull, afraid of dropping her, afraid of crib death and monsters in the closet, afraid of all the things that can go wrong. But this baby is different. This baby was born knowing how to dance. If you dropped this baby she'd land on her feet and start dancing, not missing a beat. Or maybe she'd just float, her feet never touching the ground.

You'll notice that the baby and I don't worry much about talking. That humming of hers, that cat's purr set to music, I just don't know why you'd need more than that. Oh, there are some songs, I suppose, that seem to require lyrics—"Somewhere Over the Rainbow," for instance, one of her favorites—but in such cases the baby supplies her own words. They change each time she sings a song. In carefree moods she likes vowels—words like *ayo* and *ooyee*. When she is feeling puzzled or rebellious, she makes up words with lots of *k*'s and *t*'s. Mostly, she's too happy to need words at all.

She discovers pearls in the seashells she collects. We keep them in a glass bowl to make into a necklace when she grows up. But that's for later. For now, it's enough for the baby to run her tiny starfish hands through the pearls, to feel their smooth coolness. The pearls make a soft click as they bump against each other. The baby likes the sound; she smiles and makes up a song to go with the sound of pearls clicking together in a glass bowl. The baby is carefree today, and so the words are mostly *aah* and *ohhee* and *orr*. Those are the lyrics. When she sings the pearl song tomorrow, the words will be different, or maybe tomorrow she won't need words, just humming.

The baby wears seashells on her dancing feet. She is pure sound, the sound of waves, and each night I hear her sing herself to sleep.

The Bride's Lover

Pictures he takes:

 —Amy, looking radiant (that word invented for brides), standing by the trumpet vine. The flaming trumpet-shaped flowers set off the gold streaks in her rich brown hair. If Matt took one hundred thousand pictures of Amy, he could never do her justice, never get her *right*, never express the depth of his love for her. His unselfish, let's-still-be-friends love, which is, after all, his chief motive for volunteering to be the official photographer at her wedding.

 —Amy and Warren, together. By the trumpet vine, by the cake, by the rose trellis, by the champagne table. Matt focuses on Warren's bulging Adam's apple, on his skinny wrists. He'd like to use a special lens that would zoom in on the worst of Warren's features, revealing to Amy (the camera doesn't lie) what a terrible mistake she has made in marrying this man. Though, Matt thinks sourly, Amy won't care what Warren looks like in the pictures as long as *she* looks good. All brides are beautiful on their wedding day, Matt thinks. Matt is full of clichés about brides today.

—Amy's uncle Hugh, over by the dahlias getting smashed on Chandon. Matt takes a shot of Hugh talking to himself, and it's going to look fine when it comes out, it's going to look like Hugh having a nice normal conversation with somebody who just happens to be out of the frame.

—To get it over with, a picture of Dr. and Mrs. Giovanni, whom Matt despises, possibly even more than they despise him. Amy's landlords, the Giovannis have not only rented her their downstairs garden apartment dirt cheap (she's the only tenant in San Francisco who's had her rent *lowered* over the years), they have semi-adopted her as the beloved daughter they never had. They cheered from the sidelines when Amy threw Matt over for Warren, and they look so smug today that Matt would like to slug them both. Instead he poses them in front of the rose trellis. To embarrass Dr. Giovanni, who does not approve of public displays of affection, Matt instructs him to put his arm around Mrs. Giovanni. At first Dr. G. refuses, but when it looks as if Mrs. G. is going to pout or even cry, he relents sullenly. His arm lowers over her shoulders like a plank. Dr. Giovanni scowls into the camera. Matt uses a flash, which he does not need, in the hope that Dr. Giovanni is the sort of person whose eyes turn red and vampirish in flash photographs. Matt is fairly sure Dr. Giovanni *is* that sort of person.

♦

Pictures he does not take:

—Warren and Amy together, in which the top half of Warren's head is sliced off. (Though he would like to.)

—Warren and Amy together, in which Warren is braying his horse laugh and you can see right down to his tonsils. (Though he would like to.)

—Cheap shots of Warren in general.

—The Giovannis' tabby cat Myer, lurking in the bed of crimson salvia, darting up at intervals like a jack-in-the-box to grab at hummingbirds. Myer has caught two so far that Matt has witnessed, and there may well be more. The expert way Myer dispatches these tiny creatures suggests he's got a system down. The hummingbirds ought to have figured things out by now, and maybe they have but are suicidally addicted to those red flowers. Nobody appears to have noticed Myer but Matt. This isn't the kind of thing you'd want to point out to Amy just now. Amy is an animal lover of the first order—the little murders would upset her out of all proportion, especially if she is a wellspring of emotion the way brides are supposed to be. (She doesn't *seem* to be a wellspring of emotion. She seems quite cool. Matt notices her helping out the caterer, who seems harried, frantic, on the verge of nervous collapse. You would think it was the caterer's wedding day.)

—Warren's homely, ten-years-younger cousin Pierre. In a perverse way Matt would *like* to take pictures of Pierre, if only to hold them up to Amy and say, "See? This is an example of what lurks in Warren's gene pool. Suppose you have a child with Warren—a son—and he grows up to look like Pierre? To be like Pierre?" But Matt cannot bring himself to focus on Pierre, who scratches his stomach frequently and chews the hors d'oeuvres with his mouth open. Besides, if Matt took Pierre's picture, it would only encourage Pierre, who has been following Matt around relentlessly all afternoon, attaching himself to Matt the way a cat instinctively jumps onto the lap of the one allergic person in the room.

Pierre is tall and gangly, like Warren, and has pale freckled skin and an ugly mop of curly red hair. Matt does not understand the naming of Pierre ("Perkins" does not exactly suggest French ancestry), but he suspects Pierre's parents may have had an unhappy premonition of what he was going to turn out like and were trying to head off fate by giving him a sophisticated and interesting name. Pierre has flunked out of two colleges and this summer is trying to redeem himself via a biology course at City College, in which his main project is a research experiment on insect vision. The project involves installing beetles in shoe boxes, with flash cards at one end, and seeing whether the beetles crawl toward the designs on the flash cards, or respond in any observable way. The flash cards are painted with straight lines, wavy lines, and dots. Pierre has explained the details of his experiment in excruciating, monotone detail, the way a child would explain the plot of a monster movie.

One of Matt's more satisfying fantasies involves Pierre flunking out of college for the third time, and Pierre's father shipping him off, as punishment, to live in the country with Warren and Amy. Matt wonders if Amy has noticed that Warren and Pierre, when they laugh, make the same identical neighing sound. He doesn't know how she could fail to have noticed, but just in case, he thinks that before the day is over he will try to find a subtle way to point it out to her.

Besides the insect vision project, Pierre has other equally useless interests and talents. He owns a special saw, so that he can create his own jigsaw puzzles out of balsa wood. He can play a xylophone. He can balance atop a metal wastebasket, and then walk that wastebasket across a room.

◆

It is a beautiful afternoon—late afternoon on a late summer day, a fresh breeze blowing in off San Francisco Bay—Matt's favorite time of day, of season. Amy's garden (even the Giovannis call it

Amy's garden, she has done so much with it, pruned and weeded and mulched) has never looked more lush and full. The trumpet vine, you can almost hear it sounding. The rose trellis, so carefully trained against the back of the house. The salvia . . . well, never mind the salvia with its morbid secret. And fronting all the flower beds, the fragrant, white sweet alyssum, started from seed in Amy's kitchen window. A scent so delicate Matt might never have noticed it if Amy hadn't pointed it out to him. Senses heightened, Matt can smell not only the sweet alyssum, but the sharp, salt smell of the ocean, though San Francisco Bay is several miles away—only one square of it visible from the Giovannis' second-story deck.

The hours he's spent here, in this garden, reading the *Chronicle* and drinking coffee with Amy on Sunday mornings, drinking lemonade in the afternoon, helping her stake the delphiniums, train the trumpet vine. Wine on the patio, watching the last sunlight glint the roses, the day turning into blue-gray dusk, fog rolling in, talking about whether to go out for dinner, whether to stay in. Matt had loved that garden—loved it without realizing it would one day be the setting for Amy's wedding to Warren Perkins. Warren Perkins, who is going to take Amy away from this garden, this city, her cozy apartment—take her away to Grass Valley to live in some log cabin and start up a law practice where the townsfolk pay him in ears of corn.

◆

"So," says Dr. Giovanni, "how's it going, Matthew?" He stands beside Matt, balancing his plate and his glass of champagne, crunching celery, unaware of—or more likely he doesn't care— how obnoxious a noise he's making. With his I'm-always-right manner and his shock of white hair, there's no escaping Dr. G.

"It's going fine," says Matt, gritting his teeth. He hates Dr. Giovanni. He edges away and takes several shots of Francie, Amy's eleven-year-old niece cast in the role of flower girl. Matt feels sorry for her; Francie's too old for the part, and she knows it. There she is, dolled up in pink lace and organdy, an aging movie star trying to pass for an ingenue. He takes a lot of pictures of her, hoping for just one in which she won't look sullen. Matt's a good illusionist, but he does not have the power to transform a sulky, big-for-her-age eleven-year-old into a dainty flower girl.

Dr. Giovanni never says, "How's it going, Matthew?" without having something in mind. "How's the business end of all this shaping up?" he asks, waving dismissively at Matt's Nikon. His eyes, like the eyes of a buzzard, glitter and dart.

"Fine."

"How's the Lamaze thing, specifically?"

"Fine."

"Glad to hear it," says Dr. Giovanni. "Glad I could be of service."

Thanks to Dr. Giovanni's putting in a word for him a year ago, when he was still going with Amy, Matt landed the rather plum job—plum for a freelancer, anyway—of taking pictures for an updated book on the Lamaze method which an obstetrician friend of Dr. Giovanni's is coauthoring. The job involves taking pictures of baby Lamaze graduates being lowered into vats of warm water. The babies have to look contented or the shot's no good. At this moment, Matt has hundreds of negatives of contented and not-so-contented babies hanging in his darkroom. He's going to have to do something about them eventually. To hear him talk, Giovanni has put his entire professional reputation on the line by recommending Matt for this job. Which may have something to do with the fact that Matt is probably never going to finish the project.

Matt does not want to take another picture of a baby, in or out of a vat of warm water, in his life. He doesn't want to *see* another picture of a baby, or the baby itself. Especially not the baby itself. You have a baby, you take a chance the baby will end up like Pierre, with no skills other than training beetles to recognize patterns on flash cards.

In reply to his father's protests that he's wasting his time and ought to be doing something constructive, Pierre is reported to have said, "All time is wasted time. No work is constructive." Nothing—not even being a doctor or a priest or a country lawyer—matters in the long run, said Pierre, since we are all going to die anyway.

"You play your cards right and that job could lead to something," Dr. Giovanni goes on, just the way Matt knew he would. Matt takes another shot of Francie, an unfortunate one. Her eyes widen in shock; she has noticed Myer. Now there are three tiny notches on Myer's gun.

"Mommy," cries Francie, and runs out of the frame of the picture.

Matt decides to take a break from wedding pictures, because the temptation to shoot the back of Dr. Giovanni's red fat neck or Mrs. Giovanni's slip (a good half-inch of it showing beneath her powder-blue dress) is becoming overpowering.

He puts the camera in its bag and heads for the champagne, taking a circuitous route to avoid Pierre, who is at the hors d'oeuvres table popping shrimp into his mouth like so many potato chips. Pierre, of course, spots Matt and heads right over.

"So," says Pierre, his mouth full of shrimp. "You're not taking pictures anymore."

"Not at the moment," says Matt. Pierre has a habit of pointing out the obvious.

"I've been thinking of taking up photography," Pierre says, and waits expectantly. Apparently Matt is supposed to react like a proud father who's been trying for years to talk his reluctant son into following in the family business. "I mean, how hard could it be, right?" Pierre continues.

Matt goes for the champagne.

Pierre follows. "'Course I'd hate to give up biology. Maybe I could do a double major—biology and photography. Maybe I could get one of those microscopic cameras, take close-up pictures of my insects. You know, like those ones you see in *National Geographic*? You have any idea how much one of those cameras would cost? I could probably get my dad to spring for one if it wasn't too much."

"You can't get a double major in anything if you keep flunking out," says Matt dourly. This is his first champagne of the afternoon, and he is surprised by how good it tastes. He likes champagne. He likes to take little sips of it and hold them in his mouth before swallowing. Champagne makes the inside of his cheeks numb. He likes that.

"That tone of your voice—it's just like the way Dr. Giovanni talks to *you*," says Pierre accusingly. "Talks *down* to you."

Pierre is right. This is the only time Matt can remember Pierre saying anything remotely perceptive—but Pierre undercuts the moment instantly by beginning to whine. "I might not flunk out if anybody ever gave me a *chance*, if anybody ever gave me credit. Will you let me take a few pictures? Why not?" he pleads, sing-song, anticipating Matt's refusal.

Matt shrugs. He has taken all the obligatory pictures, and it will be downhill from here. The wedding cake has been hacked to pieces. It reads:

CONGRA   AM   WAR

The shrimp platter is nearly empty; Uncle Hugh is too full of champagne for any pictures of him to fool anybody; Francie has spilled grape soda on her pink organdy dress. Even the trumpet vine flowers are starting to droop.

"Please can I take some pictures?" says Pierre.

"Why not?" says Matt. He hands over the camera bag with a magnanimous, offhand gesture, as though it does not represent his entire life savings, as though none of it matters. Giving his camera over to Pierre, he has the sudden sense that he is throwing his life away. But that's ridiculous—and anyway, it's too late to change his mind, because Pierre's face lights up like a child's. "No kidding?" The tone of Pierre's voice is like nothing Matt has ever heard out of him—light, exuberant, not the kind of relentless, aggressive enthusiasm Pierre exhibits for his usual doomed-to-defeat projects. "I'll be really careful!" Pierre shouts over his shoulder, a promise that sends chills down Matt's neck.

There's Amy, radiant (that word again), fresh, and lovely in a flower-print dress of some gauzy, light-cottony material, not a wedding sort of dress at all, not white or cream or silk. A demure, unbridelike dress with a dropped waist and a full longish skirt. A dress that would swirl around her if she danced, or if Warren picked her up and spun her around—something he would never do, of course.

The diamond glints on her hand.

Matt steps closer, listens in on a discussion she is having with John and Tom, the Giovannis' next-door neighbors, about the goldfish pond they have recently installed in their back garden. It seems that the pond, put in at great expense with the advice and counsel of a landscape architect, has turned out to be a horrific mistake. Not only does it attract raging hordes of mosquitoes, but the raccoons like it too.

"Raccoons are cute, though," says Amy.

"They're eating the goldfish," says John. "They're going through the garbage. We found a banana skin floating in the pond just this morning. The damn things go through the garbage to find food, and then they wash it in the goldfish pond. *And* they eat the goldfish."

"The goldfish pond has been a disaster," Tom agrees.

"I'm so glad I didn't try to talk the Giovannis into putting one in," Amy says. "I was thinking of it. I liked the idea of yours so much."

"The idea of things," says Tom glumly. "The idea of things."

"We're thinking about suing the company that put it in," John says. "They never mentioned a word about mosquitoes."

"This city," says Tom, making some sort of leap in logic that Matt does not fully understand. "You're lucky you're getting out. Truly lucky."

"Yes," says Amy, her tone neutral. "I think you're right. It's time. I'm pressing my luck, staying here. Do you know, I think my apartment is the only one left on this block that hasn't been burglarized?"

John and Tom shake their heads. Their home was robbed just two months ago. The VCR was stolen, plus an expensive crystal figurine they'd bought on a trip to Ireland.

Something occurs to Tom. He says, "I'm wondering now if our burglar was one of those guys who put in the goldfish pond. He had access to the house, you know. Now that I think of it, he was always coming inside to get drinks of water, so he said."

Matt's tired of letting Myer get away with murder. He reaches into the salvia and hauls out the fat tabby. Myer, usually so placid and good-natured, spits and hisses.

"Fair's fair," he tells Myer in a low voice. "You're shooting hummingbirds in a rain barrel, and on Amy's wedding day. Shame on you."

Myer bares his teeth, lets out a low growl. There are pinprick holes, one for each of Myer's claws, in Matt's right wrist.

He thrusts Myer into Mrs. Giovanni's arms. "I think you ought to get him inside," he tells her. "He's wiping out an entire tribe of hummingbirds. He's putting them on the endangered list."

Mrs. G. looks affronted (and what for? Matt hasn't accused *her*, personally, of murdering hummingbirds). She hustles Myer away, throwing Matt a look of pure dislike over her shoulder.

Amy is watching. She has her hostess antennae out, picking up bad vibes, which aren't allowed on a wedding day. She says something to John and Tom. They glance at him—pityingly, he thinks. They nod, hug her, move away. Amy joins Matt.

"What was that all about?" she says.

"You look radiant," Matt tells her. "Just like a bride."

"Cut it out, Matt," she says. "I mean it." Her diamond ring catches the sun.

"I'm not being sarcastic. You didn't think I was being sarcastic, did you? You look beautiful," he says softly.

She smiles, looking tired for the first time all afternoon. "Thanks." She plunks down into one of the lawn chairs, and he pulls one up near her. For a moment he's able to shut out the other guests. They've sat this way, across from each other, many times in this garden. "I know why you volunteered to take the pictures today," she says. "And I know why I wanted you to. It's a way of trying to make everything all right. You and I," she says, and smiles again, still looking tired, "that's our big problem. We always want everything to be all right. That's why we stayed together so much longer than we should have. We tried to piece things back together when they were falling apart."

"They weren't falling apart."

"See what I mean? Matt. They were falling apart. We had fights that ended with you spending the night in your darkroom, for God's sake."

15

But what Matt remembers is not that. He has a sudden image—bright and sharp as if he'd taken a picture that first day and carried it around with him since. Amy, taking cover from the rain, sitting in Henrietta's, that pickup bar she hasn't yet figured out is a pickup bar. She looks bewildered, raindrops glistening on her bangs, and she glances up at him and smiles, not coy or flirtatious, just nice, and a little shy. She's new in the city, like he is. Both of them, new as two pennies. It's four years ago. They recognize each other for what they are, that rainy afternoon in Henrietta's—two orphans of the storm.

"I just don't get it," Matt says, making a sweeping gesture of the house, the garden, the little square of bay that they can't see now but *could* see if they were up on the Giovannis' second-story deck. "How can you give all this up? How can you give up your life?"

She sighs. "Matt."

"How can you give up the garden?"

"I'm not going to *not* get married on account of a garden. A garden that isn't even mine." Then she says, suddenly, "The foundation of the Giovannis' house is sagging, do you know that? They just told me. They just found out themselves. They said they're going to sell the house. So you see. I probably couldn't live here much longer even if I wanted to. They'll probably sell the place for four hundred thousand dollars, even though whoever buys it will know the foundation's rotten. That's how it is in this town. That's what people do. They pay four hundred thousand dollars for a house with a rotten foundation. You know that perfectly well. They're crazy. You have this rosy glow, Matt, this unrealistic view of it all. And of me. It's just a tiny apartment in a falling-down house in an iffy neighborhood. I'm just a woman who wants to get married and probably have babies. I want to go and live in the country and start my own garden, grow vegetables."

"I don't believe you. I can always tell when you're lying to yourself."

"Matt. Cut it out. It's too late for all this. I'm going to go and live in the country, with Warren. Tomorrow the movers are coming. I'm leaving, Matt."

"I know. You don't have to keep telling me. I know."

◆

Four years ago Matt was twenty-four, and Amy was twenty-three. Two medium-sized fish from two small ponds—Amy from a little town in Ohio, not the first notion of what she wanted to do with her life, just desperate to get out of the Midwest and see the world. Matt, from a little town in eastern Nevada, puffed up from winning a couple of local photography contests and from the respectful way the customers in the camera shop where he worked listened to his advice about lighting and f-stops. Those people thought he was a genius. It had gone to his head, and even now that he's figured out what the competition's like, and that he's probably not as good as he thought he was, it's too late. He's hooked.

Both Matt and Amy had the same response when anybody asked where they were from. "A little town in Ohio that you've probably never heard of." "A little town in Nevada—you wouldn't have heard of it." Usually they were exactly right—the person *hadn't* heard of it.

Both of them came to the big city, to see the world, make their fortunes. Silly.

Except it had worked, more or less. When they thought "fortune," they had something modest in mind. Amy got a job in one of those stylish florist shops on Sacramento Street. She hadn't even applied for it. She'd just walked in one day to buy some flowers to cheer herself up. Things happened to her that way—the job, the garden apartment of the Giovannis'. She took to the city as if it were her natural habitat, and now it seemed strange that it was she, not Matt, who was leaving.

The magic had worked for him too, though, at least for a while. There was always somebody who knew somebody who needed some photography work done. Matt couldn't even keep track, anymore, of the number of jobs that had come his way just through striking up conversations with people at North Beach coffeehouses. It was only when he did the math, figured up his profits against his expenses, that he realized what a small-town boy he still was at heart. He couldn't bring himself to charge as much for his work as he knew he should. But even that didn't matter. The string of studio apartments he'd shared with mice along the way, even the condemned building in the Tenderloin where he'd camped out for three weeks—all of that was exciting, part of the allure. And of course, it was much more exciting once he met Amy. He thought of them as adventurers.

The sense of possibility, that's what Matt had loved and what, growing up in that barren Nevada town, he had never known. Every weekend he and Amy drove across the Golden Gate into Sausalito, just to see that red bridge glowing in the sun, just to see the rainbow painted on the tunnel. The end of the rainbow. They walked along Marina Boulevard at night, to watch the lights sparkling on the bay, and to peer shamelessly and without envy into the lighted windows of the expensive homes that fronted the water. One window had an ebony grand piano, so highly polished it reflected the bowl of roses sitting on it. Another window featured a full-sized carousel pony dressed in pink and yellow ribbons.

It was all exciting. The ferry ride to Tiburon cost practically nothing, and when you got there you felt like you'd traveled to an exotic foreign city. The hang gliders at Land's End, bright-colored, swooping in so close to shore you could reach up and almost touch them.

And then, out of the blue, sprang Warren, a San Francisco boy born and raised, who didn't seem to find anything magical about the place at all. And suddenly, it seemed that all Matt heard from people—on the bus, at parties, in elevators—was how things had changed. A pall had come over the city. Everyone felt it. Earthquakes and fires, and everyone knew someone who had died of AIDS. There was the traffic, worse every day, and taxes, and you couldn't afford to own your own home, you couldn't afford to live, and what was the point of it all?

Matt blamed Warren, exclusively, for the way the city had changed its attitude toward itself.

Warren wanted to take his law practice out into the country. A country lawyer. He wanted to buy some land—a vineyard, maybe, a plum orchard. And Amy's Ohio roots kicked in. She wanted that too, all of a sudden. Just all of a sudden.

♦

"How much have you told Warren?" he asks her now. "About us, I mean."

"Haven't we been over this?" She looks more puzzled than irritated.

It's true they have been over it, but Matt says, "I mean at the beginning. When you first met him. When you were first explaining your life to him."

She shrugs. "I told him that we'd sort of lived together but not quite—never quite made that final step of pooling our possessions, sharing a bathroom. That you always had your own place to go to when we had a fight." A silence.

"What else?" he says finally.

She sighs. "That we mentioned marriage, but always in such vague terms I was never sure if marriage was what either of us was talking about. That we broke up a lot because we could never figure out how to be happy together."

"So," he says. "It's not just that he's being noble about all this. He's not jealous at all. You made it sound like there was never anything to be jealous of, like I was just some guy in your life who barely counted."

"I should have known you were going to do this." She closes her eyes and rubs them. "I did know you would do this. Down deep, I knew it."

"We were happy," he says.

She opens her eyes then, and she doesn't look tired anymore. She looks mad, fed up. "Matt," she says. "I know this probably appeals to your sense of irony and all that, but I don't think my wedding reception is the proper occasion for us to be discussing why you and I shouldn't have broken up."

"Proper occasion," says Matt scornfully. "Proper."

"Yes, 'proper.' It's my wedding, Matt. I want it to be nice. I do." Two spots of color have appeared on her cheeks. She says it again, her voice trembling. "I want it to be nice."

"I'm sorry, Amy," he says. He is always doing this, hurting her without meaning to. Her leaving him has nothing to do with Warren. He knows this. It was his own impatience, his drive for some sort of stupid notion of success. Too many hours spent in his darkroom, his brain scrambled with chemicals and black-and-white images, so that when he came out into the light and the air the change was too great, like somebody surfacing too fast after scuba diving. It made him irritable, abrupt, and cranky, unlike Warren, who's so generous, so easygoing.

Matt's eyes flicker to Warren. He realizes he's had Warren in view all along, out of the corner of his eye. He's been tracking him without being aware of it. But Warren's safely ensconced in a basking-in-approval conversation with Dr. and Mrs. Giovanni, who love him, and he doesn't look over.

"I wonder if I'd hate Warren if you weren't marrying him. If I just met him at a party and didn't know he had anything to do with you," Matt says thoughtfully. "I think I'd hate him. Pretty sure I would."

Amy sighs. "Matt."

"What I miss," says Matt, leaning forward, "is the sense of possibility. That's what I miss. You know what I mean?"

Amy leans forward, too. She looks at him, sad, not understanding but obviously wishing she did.

And Pierre comes along and takes a picture of them, just like that.

◆

In a minute Warren lopes over. He's seen the look Matt gave him, after all, and has taken it for an invitation. Or maybe he's been tracking Matt the same way Matt's been tracking him, subconsciously. "You're monopolizing my wife," says Warren heartily. Warren's got a spot of wedding-cake frosting on his tie. Amy probably finds this sort of thing endearing.

"I sat down about a minute and a half ago to talk to her," says Matt irritably. "I'm not monopolizing her."

Warren laughs, as though Matt has made a joke. "I wouldn't blame you, even if you were. It's all right."

"No," says Matt, and his eyes flick to Amy. "It isn't all right."

There's a pause, and then Warren says it too. "No," he says, softly. "I guess it isn't all right." Apparently Warren is feeling the same way he is, wishing they could go off in an alley and fight or something, or, more accurately, wishing Matt had never been invited to the wedding in the first place. Wishing they didn't have to play out this civilized game of trying to be friends.

Pierre is about to take a picture of the three of them, but he thinks better of it, lowers the camera. Matt can see the wheels turning in Pierre's head, can see him putting it all together, Matt's jealousy and resentment, Warren trying to make peace in his bumbling way, Amy's embarrassment at being caught in the middle.

"Sometimes weddings just go on too long," Amy says to no one in particular. "Don't they. I've noticed it before, but it's something that never occurred to me when I was planning my own." She has that tone in her voice Matt knows well. Any minute now she could start crying. Warren, amazingly enough, doesn't seem to recognize the danger signals. But maybe it's not that Warren is dense. To be fair, Matt thinks, it's more likely that Warren has never pushed Amy to the edge of tears, the way Matt, over the past four years, seems to have become an expert at doing.

"I'll throw my bouquet," she says. "That's what I'll do. That's what they do at the end of a wedding. Like passing on the torch or something, isn't it?" Her tone is vague, distracted. She stands up. Pierre looks at Matt. He doesn't say a word, for once, but he clutches the camera close to his heart. His eyes are so eloquent and pleading Matt has to smile. He shrugs. "Sure," he says. "If it's okay with Amy."

But Amy is past caring. "Fine," she says. Matt doubts whether she even knows what she's agreeing to.

Her bouquet has been gathered from the garden—rosebuds and forget-me-nots. It's so fresh and fragrant that when Amy picks it up from the table, a bee zooms in and buries itself in it, ecstatic—but she doesn't seem to notice. Bees would never sting Amy, anyway.

"Shoot it at a high shutter speed," Warren advises Pierre. "So you don't get a blur when she throws the bouquet."

"Actually," Matt begins, and is pleased when Pierre stops and waits to hear what Matt will say. He's annoyed at Warren—typical of Warren to horn in, giving advice on a subject he knows nothing about. "Actually," he says again, "if I were you, I *wouldn't* shoot it at a high shutter speed. I think you *want* a hint of blur, a feeling of motion—otherwise the shot will look artificial."

Warren holds up both hands in surrender. "Sorry," he says, "you're the doctor," and laughs his horse laugh.

The crystal-clear shot Warren suggested is exactly the shot Matt himself probably *would* have taken, without thinking. When in doubt he usually goes for clarity, and he probably would have done it in this case too. Of course Warren has no way of knowing that.

Feeling eyes upon him, he glances up. Myer, imprisoned in an upstairs room—probably Mrs. G.'s bedroom—is looking down on him from the windowsill, furious, plotting revenge.

"*You* better set the camera," Pierre says, uncharacteristically timid, and thrusts it at Matt. So, as Amy gathers together all the more-or-less-marriageable females in the crowd and positions them, Matt focuses, chooses the appropriate aperture.

"Let her rip," he says to Pierre, and hands over the Nikon. Amy, hearing him, takes this as her cue too.

Pierre clutches the camera, stares desperately into the viewfinder, as Amy throws the bouquet in a broad and lovely backhand arc, her gauzy dress and hair swirling. She ends up on tiptoe, both arms flung high and wide. It's an astonishing gesture, a wistful, reaching gesture. Behind his left shoulder, Matt hears the *click-click-click* of the Nikon—Pierre shooting furiously—and he crosses his fingers for one good shot of that miraculous throw. The flowers sail across the sky.

Then it's over, and Amy looks embarrassed, as though she has just broken into a jig, or put a lampshade on her head in front of all these people.

The wedding bouquet has been caught by Francie the flower girl. A bit too athletic, Amy overshot her mark, and Francie, a sleepy outfielder squinting in the sun, has caught the ball by pure mistake. In one accidental motion, she has transformed herself from flower girl to the equally inappropriate role of bride-to-be, and Matt has to wonder whether this will always be Francie's destiny—to be caught in some all-wrong in-between state.

Pierre digs his elbow into Matt's ribs. "What do you think?" he demands. "Pretty good, don't you think? If these turn out good, I bet my dad might buy me one of those microscopic cameras. How much do you think they cost? How much?"

"Probably a lot," Matt replies. "I honestly don't know." He wonders if his own dreams for success are as futile as Pierre's insect-vision dreams. He remembers thinking that if he just got that Nikon (nothing else would do, not an Olympus or a Canon or even a Hasselblad), everything would fall into place.

So Amy has thrown the bouquet to the wrong person, and isn't that the way it always works? Though, could there ever be a right person, under such circumstances? A person who at a particular moment has her hope chest all filled and an eager groom-to-be waiting in the wings?

The bouquet-throwing is the sign for everyone to go home, though they don't. They hang around for a while longer, missing their cue.

◆

Pictures he does not take of the end of the wedding:

—Dr. and Mrs. Giovanni hugging Amy. Dr. G., of course, behaves like he's never hugged anybody in his life, and maybe he hasn't. Watching him make this gesture so awkwardly and stiffly, Matt realizes that Amy is right to leave. It's all baloney, her being like a daughter to the Giovannis. If she stayed, they'd sell this rotting house and her apartment with it, right out from under her. She's not their daughter; she's their tenant. They give her a break on the rent because of the garden work she does, but she still has to come up with a check every month. That benevolent approval she enjoys would fly right out the window if she ever missed a payment.

—Myer, strolling out to the garden, smug and free. It's twilight and the hummingbirds have gone to bed, that's probably Mrs. G.'s thinking, her reason for springing him. Amy, trusting and innocent of Myer's crimes, picks him up and holds his furry cheek against her cheek. He purrs, the hypocrite.

—Uncle Hugh, weeping a little, from drunkenness and regret.

—Amy, when she thinks no one is watching, taking Warren's hand, tracing the lines of his palm as though she were reading his fortune. It's one of those gestures you have to recognize for what it is, a gesture of love. That simple. That tracing of her finger across his palm makes it all clear that Amy has married Warren because she loves him, and that the two of them are moving out of the city because that is what they want to do.

—The evening fog rolling in from the ocean, though Matt would like to try just one shot, for practice. The San Francisco fog is one reason Matt can't imagine himself living anywhere else. He's always trying to capture its mystical elusive quality on film. It never comes out quite right, but he's had enough near successes to make him keep trying. He notices that the smell of the fog has completely obscured the delicate scent of the sweet alyssum. The wedding is over. It's time to go home.

And after the guests have gone, and tomorrow after the

movers have come to take away her furniture, Amy and Warren will drive right out of the fog, forever, heading east.

Not Matt, though. He's going to stay. That he's going to stay is as true as anything he knows. That fog, the sharp salt smell of the ocean. The smell of longing and nostalgia. The smell he will always associate with losing Amy. A smell he loves, in spite of himself.

♦

In fact, Matt doesn't take any more pictures at all that day, after Pierre hands back the Nikon. Later, when he goes to the dark-room, he will develop the last roll of film—Pierre's roll—first. Sure enough, there will be one picture of Amy throwing her bouquet that is perfect, as good as anything Matt himself could do. She is all fluid motion—dress and hair swirling, a long, late-summer afternoon shadow dancing beneath her. The bouquet sails through the air, already out of the frame. It's a heartbreakingly beautiful photograph. It might be the photograph of a woman flinging pearls into the sea.

Our New Life

A three-day cross-country bus trip from Lincoln, Nebraska, and here I was, new in town. Santa Cruz, the town I'd chosen to adopt because how could you ever be unhappy in a town with an ocean and a boardwalk? Even on a foggy day (not that fog has ever bothered me, I have an accommodating nature and I take things as they come, which has always been one of my problems), you'd have someplace to go, a walk you could take. You could buy cotton candy on the boardwalk, follow the tracks of sandpipers on the beach.

I'd barely unpacked my bags at my no-ocean-view, pay-by-the-week seedy motel when I looked out my window and there, kitty-corner across the street, I saw a sign for "Irene Post, Ph.D."

Now. Here's the thing. Irene Post had been my therapist back in Lincoln, the one who'd urged me to make this change, the one who'd said, "Why don't you think about moving?" Irene's advice tended to be couched in gentle, nonthreatening terms like that: just think about it, just get used to the idea, just do a touch of creative visualization. And before I knew it, presto, here I was.

But here she was too, apparently. That wasn't part of the plan.

Her sign was a whimsical sign, very unlike the no-nonsense sign she'd had outside her office on 14th Street in Lincoln. This one was painted in calligraphy, with a picture of a sand dollar beside her name. This could be a different Irene Post, of course, except it did seem so like Irene to use a sand *dollar* for a logo as a subliminal reminder that her services did not come cheap.

One reason I stopped going to Irene, back in Lincoln, was that she raised her prices from eighty to eighty-five dollars an hour. I didn't complain at the time, but I did think, *hmm*, and ever after that I began subconsciously to search for reasons to think I was cured. Another reason I stopped going to Irene was that Lincoln, though not a small town, seemed like a small town. Occasionally I would run into her socially, and how, exactly, do you talk to your therapist at a cocktail party, someone who knows all your secrets but can't let on? Especially when there I'd be, caught with a glass of wine in my hand after I'd spent the previous week's session vowing to quit drinking for good, starting immediately. I'd begun to think that Lincoln wasn't a big enough city for the two of us.

Now here she was. In Santa Cruz.

I thought what the hell, walked across the street, and knocked on her office door. She answered. It was Irene all right, but she had cut her hair short like a boy's and dyed it red.

"Irene," I said.

She peered at me as if she didn't know who I was, which I suppose I can understand even though I *had* bared my soul to her once a week for six solid months. I looked different; that was why she didn't recognize me. I'd cut my hair too. It took her a moment, but then she said, "Polly!" with a definite exclamation point in her tone, but I didn't know if the exclamation point meant pleasure, or surprise, or dismay.

"This is just a social visit," I said hurriedly. I didn't want to be slapped for an eighty-five-dollar session. I had just spent all my therapy money on bus fare and seedy-motel-room charges. "I didn't even bring my checkbook." This was a lie. I had it right there in my purse. Of course it was my old checkbook from Lincoln, and so far nobody in Santa Cruz would accept out-of-state checks, so probably Irene wouldn't either.

When she heard what I had to say about the checkbook, I thought for a minute Irene was going to shut the door in my face. I could see her considering it.

I had never liked the way Irene did business. I thought she should have accepted Visa and Mastercard, or at the very least sent a bill at the end of the month. But she didn't want to be bothered with those kinds of bookkeeping details. She liked—she *insisted*—on being paid at the beginning of each session, by check or cash. So our financial transactions always had a furtive tone. It felt like paying her under the table for doing something illegal.

"Come in," she said finally, and opened the door a crack wider, just enough for me to slip inside.

Her office was nice but tiny, with a view of the ocean, though today pretty much all you could see out the window was fog. The walls were painted a creamy glowing white, and on a little table were three identical peach-colored vases with no flowers in them. The vases had the same glow that the walls had. The effect was cheerful and sparkly, even on this foggy day.

I couldn't take my eyes off Irene's hair. I'd left my own hair behind in Nebraska, after a session spent talking about how insecure I was and how my whole identity was wrapped up in the idea that my long hair was the only desirable quality I possessed. Why don't you just *think* about cutting it? Irene had said. It will grow back, you know; it's not an irrevocable decision. Why don't you visualize yourself walking down the sidewalk with short swingy hair? So I cut it, and sure enough, the very next day a man I worked with, a man who'd barely said hello to me in the past, asked me out for lunch. It turned out we had nothing in common, and got on each other's nerves, but still.

Thinking about this made me feel warm and grateful toward Irene. "You were a good therapist," I told her. "You offered actual advice instead of just sitting there in the kind of silence—you know the kind I mean—that is meant to seem nonjudgmental but instead feels like just the opposite. I liked the fact that you offered practical advice. 'Why don't you think about cutting your hair? Why don't you think about changing jobs? Why don't you think about keeping an anger journal and writing down all those homicidal feelings you have toward your ex-husband?' I appreciated your advice. You cured me. I believe that."

"No one is ever cured," she said. She spoke curtly, and that made me remember how abrupt she could sometimes be, to the point of rudeness, and the warm feeling I had toward her evaporated.

Irene had advised me to cut my hair, and I had. But she hadn't said a word about dyeing it. And here she'd gone and cut hers much shorter than mine—a boyish, feathery cut, probably just exactly right for the ocean. The wind could blow and toss it around while she was jogging, and it wouldn't matter. But I didn't know if Irene jogged. Or if she jogged *now*, but hadn't jogged *then* when she was back in Nebraska.

"Why did you do it?" I asked, but I wasn't sure whether I meant "Why did you cut your hair?" or "Why did you dye your hair?" or "Why did you move to Santa Cruz?" or some other fundamental, existential "why" question for which no real answer existed. In any case, it didn't matter because Irene ignored the question. She waved her arm in a wide, expansive gesture that apparently meant I should sit down. There were no chairs, however, just some pillows tossed haphazardly on the floor and a lumpy-looking futon mattress. This was nothing at all like the office Irene had had in Nebraska. There wasn't even a box of Kleenex to be seen. In Nebraska, she'd always had Kleenex at the ready. I'd personally made my way through several boxes.

I sat down and tried to make myself comfortable on the cushions. During my one semester in college I'd taken a yoga class and had actually enjoyed sitting on the floor cross-legged, but I hadn't done it for some time and I was not pleased (but also not surprised) to discover that my body wasn't as limber as it had been back then.

"Would you like some coffee?" she said. "A soda?" She had always offered such refreshments at the beginning of our sessions (right after the furtive exchange of money), and I had always appreciated the offer. It seemed like a nice, gracious-hostess thing to do, a gesture meant to put you at ease and give the impression that the two of you were just settling down to a nice friendly chat over coffee. (Of course, it was a hypocritical gesture, too, was it not? Because the cup of coffee cost you eighty-five dollars, and it was *not* just a nice friendly chat. I suppose this is the kind of basic decision that therapists must make as they're finishing up their Ph.D.'s and getting ready to hang out their shingles: Will I be the kind of therapist who offers coffee, or will I not?)

I said yes to the idea of coffee, but Irene made no move to get any, and indeed I noticed no coffeepot or coffee cups anywhere in the room. In one graceful motion she sank down into a full lotus position on one of the floor pillows. I was jealous.

"When you find yourself giving people the same advice over and over," Irene said to me, "you start to think, wait a minute, what's going on here? Do you see what I'm getting at?"

I didn't. "The same advice? You mean you advised other people to move to Santa Cruz? To cut their hair? But how can that be? Those were my ideas. Santa Cruz is a place I've dreamed about living in since I was a child."

Irene gazed out the window. It should by all rights have been a gloomy and depressing day, but those peach-colored vases and the creamy white walls glowed with their own luminescence. It was a pleasant room. "What I have observed after years of practice," said Irene ponderously (as though she were some wise gray elder with eons of experience, when I know for a fact that she went back to school to get her degree only after her children were grown), "is that people don't take enough risks. They do only safe things. They fly, yes, but only in their dreams. I found myself getting snappish when my patients would tell me their flying dreams. Well, what do you *think* they mean, lunkhead, I wanted to say, and sometimes did say, though not in such rude terms, of course."

"Oh, you could be rude," I told her. "You were capable of rudeness."

"What in heaven's name do you *think* the dream is trying to tell you? I would say to them. It's telling you to fly. *To fly.* Do you need to pay a therapist eighty dollars an hour to figure that out?"

"Eighty-five," I corrected, but she didn't respond.

I wondered if I myself had been one of those patients who had so irritated Irene with their flying dreams. I couldn't remember having related any of my dreams, but that didn't mean it hadn't happened. Mostly, I remembered talking to Irene about practical matters, not dreams. An unhappy marriage to a faithless man, a dead-end job drawing up insurance policies and typing threatening letters to people who were behind in their premiums.

"Going to you was the riskiest thing I'd ever done in my life,"

I told Irene now. "I couldn't afford you. I packed a lunch every day for a year to save up for your fee. I wanted to pay it myself, not put in an insurance claim. I worked for an insurance company, after all. I thought if they knew I was going to a therapist they might start looking at me skeptically. They might even fire me."

"They would have," said Irene promptly. "Insurance companies are notoriously conservative and suspicious when it comes to matters of the psyche. Pretty soon, out the door with you. Oh, they'd tell you it was for some other reason—cutbacks, downsizing—but they'd be lying."

"Not that it would have mattered," I said, "since I ended up quitting my job anyway. But still." I succeeded, with great difficulty, in maneuvering my legs into a half lotus. "Sometimes," I went on, "I'd think, this is stupid, eating peanut butter sandwiches every day so I can give the money to somebody who makes ten times as much as I do. Still, you helped me. I'll admit it."

"*Hmm*," said Irene musingly, looking out the window at the fog. "You know why I stopped practicing?"

"Stopped?" I said, shocked. "What do you mean? Why do you have that sign up?" I pointed to it out the window. The calligraphy had been skillfully done, not to mention the sand dollar. She must have paid a pretty penny for that sign.

"It doesn't say 'Irene Post, *Psychologist*,'" she said snappishly. "It just says 'Irene Post, Ph.D.' The Ph.D. could be in anything. English. Biochemistry. I worked hard for that Ph.D., and I want people to know I have one. That's all." She went on. "Here's why I stopped. I didn't feel needed. Psychotherapy is a luxury for the well-to-do. You don't see construction workers, janitors, typists running to a therapist every time they've got a problem."

"I was a typist, don't you remember? That's just what I've been talking about. I couldn't afford you. Haven't you been listening?"

"No," said Irene, sounding unrepentant. "That's another reason why I got out of the business. I listened so hard for years. I think something snapped finally. Now," she said, waving a hand breezily, "I hardly listen to anything anybody says. Little snatches—words and phrases here and there that don't make much sense."

"But what do you *do*, then?" I asked. "What do you do now that you don't have a practice?"

"Go for walks on the beach. Collect sand dollars. Dye my hair when the mood strikes. Though I might keep it this color, at least for a while. I like it. Do you agree?"

"I do." It was a luminous color—like the peach-colored vases and the sparkling white walls. She looked positively effervescent, a bottle of champagne in human form. But I was irked. The haircut had been *my* idea. How unfair of her to take my idea and go it one better. It had never even occurred to me to dye my hair. Cutting it was drastic enough—it was all I could do to creatively-visualize the act. Still, I was glad I had done it. When a breeze went by and touched my bare neck, the feeling was new and sensual.

"That's another thing," Irene said, running her fingers through her newly short, newly dyed hair. "The word 'practice.' Have you thought about the irony of that word? For eighty dollars an hour I get to *practice* on people."

"Eighty-five."

"The implication is that you just practice and practice and never get it right. There should be a final session for every patient where the therapist stops practicing. The equivalent of a piano recital."

"Well," I said, "I myself never did well at piano recitals. I usually bombed. Nerves, you know. Usually I did a lot better at my practice sessions than I did at the recitals. So maybe 'practice' is a good word. Less threatening. Less stressful." My legs in the half lotus were going to sleep. I shifted into a simple cross-legged position.

Then I remembered that Irene and I had spent several expensive sessions on this very topic of stress and how it related to my underachieving problem. I took low-level jobs, said Irene, because they were less stressful, the path of least resistance. No risk equalled no possibility of failure. As soon as she pointed out my underachieving problem and its implications, it all became clear to me. I felt like a slow-witted dog who finally, after its owners have demonstrated and prodded, catches on how to open its own dog door. It figures out that the resistance, the magnetic pull at the bottom of the door, can be broken through so easily, no trick to it at all. All it has to do is burst through the door and there it is on the other side. Freedom! It learns that it doesn't have to wait for anybody to let it out.

"I might consider that," Irene said. "And then again, I might not." I didn't know what she was referring to. This time when she ran her fingers through her hair, it stuck out all over instead of falling back into place, making her look like a mischievous nine-year-old boy. It was like being with a whole new person. Not only because of the hair but also because of the fact that she apparently no longer listened to anything anybody said. "Fish," I said, just to test her out. "Pine trees. Caribou."

She nodded. "Precisely," she said.

The fog lifted then, as if a giant invisible hand had come along and pushed it far out to sea. With the sun coming in and falling on those already-glowing white walls and peach vases and Irene's red hair, the effect was so bright I had to blink my eyes and look away.

I didn't say this to Irene because it sounded too much like the kind of thing a patient would say in a therapy session (and besides, she wouldn't have listened anyway), but I realized just then that in all my creative visualizations of Santa Cruz, I'd visualized it in fog. An underachiever even in my daydreams. A failure of nerve—I couldn't bring myself to imagine a perfect sunny day on the beach. Well, here it was in reality, a day beyond my wildest dreams. I would leave Irene's office soon, go out and walk on that beach, let the sun shine on the back of my neck.

But Irene seemed in no hurry to have me go. She settled back on her pillow. She moved from a full to a half lotus, which I was glad to see. That full lotus was nothing but showing off, in my opinion. She said, "And another thing. Guilt. Guilt and fear of risk. Those are the two big things when you practice" (her lip curled around the word) "psychotherapy. You're always trying to root out guilt. But I kept finding that I myself felt guilty. Guilty about taking people's money when all I did was sit there. Guilty about making them dependent on me. Guilty about the sneaking thought that maybe I *wanted* them dependent on me. For example," she said, "you ask me what I do. Up until a month or so ago I fed birds. I had a bird feeder right outside that window." She pointed, though it wasn't necessary. There was only the one window. "I kept a little chart. I counted how many birds came, and what kind. Then it occurred to me I was making the birds dependent on me. So I stopped feeding them. It broke my heart but I stopped. And still they come around. It's going to take a long time for it to sink in that the food's gone for good.

"Now you see," said Irene, "in this case it's only a small ethical decision. California birds are not the same as Nebraska birds. The weather is mild here—there are fruits and berries galore, not to mention sand fleas on the beach for the carnivorous ones. So they've never been truly dependent on me. They think they are, but they're not. My cracked sunflower seeds are an hors d'oeuvre, a delicacy, not a staple. Which is the way I think of people here. Nobody *needs* anything. They think they do but they don't. They live on sunshine and sea air, mineral water and fresh-squeezed orange juice. But if I had started feeding the birds back in Nebraska, in the fall with a hard winter coming on, I'd feel guilty if I stopped, and I'd be right to feel guilty. That's the thing you have to realize—sometimes you *should* feel guilty."

I yawned, and wondered if this was the way Irene had felt back when she was still practicing. It couldn't have been a lot of fun, listening to some patient blather on about birds and guilt without making any kind of sense.

"I've never had much feeling for birds myself," I said, but Irene just smiled vaguely and gazed out the window.

It was liberating, in a way, to be with someone who didn't listen—you could say anything that came into your head—but I was also beginning to find it annoying.

"Where is your husband? Where is your husband?" I asked. I thought maybe it would work if I repeated the things I particularly wanted her to hear. It seemed a good strategy; she tuned in right away.

"I left him," she said promptly. "High and dry. No sense doing things halfway. He was my safety net, and that's no good. You have to see if you can operate without a safety net or what's the point, you're not really changing anything."

"Do you miss him? Do you miss him?" But repeating the question didn't work this time, because just then a bird—a pink one—touched down on the windowsill, scratching the ledge with its tiny feet.

"You see what I mean?" sighed Irene. "Still hoping for food."

"Your husband. Do you miss him?" I asked a third time. I had met Irene's husband once, at one of those Lincoln cocktail parties. His name was Peter. He wore round glasses, and although he had a kindly face, I was taken aback to see that he had combed long strands of hair over his bald spot. I know you shouldn't make judgments about people based on such petty and superficial details, but I have trouble respecting a man who would comb his hair like that. Such obvious deception—who did he think he was fooling? A man like that would be capable of anything. Irene could come home from a hard day's work and find him in bed with her best friend, and he'd pull the sheet up over the friend's naked body and say to Irene, "What best friend?"

"You know," said Irene thoughtfully, "that's a good question. I don't miss him. Another thing to feel guilty about, I suppose. I *tell* him I miss him—we talk on the phone quite often. But he's so predictable that when anything happens I always know exactly how he'd respond, what he'd say, so I don't actually need his physical presence. 'Penny wise, pound foolish'—he says things like that. 'A fool and his money,' that sort of thing. His platitudes all have to do with money, which I suppose is reasonable given the fact that he's an accountant. Still. I don't think people should let money consume their lives, do you?"

"Easy for you to say. You make eighty-five dollars an hour."

"Made," she corrected. "Past tense." I noticed she listened when she wanted to. "You certainly do think about money a lot, don't you?" she said with an unpleasant smirk. "It's a symptom of a basically mistrustful nature."

"I think it's perfectly natural to think about things you haven't got," I told her. "I haven't got any money. You have."

"Not anymore," she said. "I've given up practicing, remember? Don't you listen?"

"Ha," I said. "I can just imagine the cushion you must have. The fat nest egg, enough rainy-day money for a typhoon. An accountant husband investing all those eighty-five-dollar hours. Still, nobody's money lasts forever. What will you do when yours runs out?" I said, just to get her goat, "I guess you can always go home to Peter."

She looked irritated, so I knew my comment had struck home. But who was she kidding? All that nonsense about risks and flying. She'd cut her hair shorter than mine and dyed it brighter, but when all was said and done she could go home and pick up her old life whenever she wanted. She'd said she didn't have a safety net but of course she did. Hadn't she just told me she and Peter spoke on the phone periodically? And didn't she look radiant in her new red hair? He with his pitiful strands combed over his vast bald head—he'd take her back in a minute. Whereas *my* husband had left *me*, not the other way around, and was now in Cincinnati married to a woman who uncannily resembled his mother. There was no going back for me.

"It's not fair," I said. "You did all the things you told *me* to do. That was *my* life. Those were *my* changes. The new town, the new haircut."

"There's no copyright on a town," she said. "You can't lay claim to a hairdo. And besides, the dye job was all my idea, you never once mentioned such a thing. I gave you good advice. It was so good I decided to take it myself." She shrugged. "So sue me." She laughed. "See? Money again. Now you've got me doing it."

"But it was *my* advice. It was meant for me."

"Well? You're taking it, aren't you? It's working, isn't it?"

"But I don't have a safety net. It has to work. I have no choice."

"Well, you see? You're luckier than I am. My circumstances were less desperate than yours. I made more money. I had the better life. I could have gone on for years quite happily, just the way I was, and so it was harder for me to change my life than for you to change yours. Braver." And she smiled at me in that faintly smug way she'd always had.

I said, "If you believe that, change places with me. Go and live in my seedy motel and let me stay here." It was important enough to say twice. "Go and live in my seedy motel—"

"I heard you the first time," she said, and tossed her head, a throwback gesture to the time when she still had hair to toss.

"So do it," I dared her.

"I will," she said curtly. Rudely.

And she did.

♦

Sometimes when I walk past the seedy motel I look up and wave, just in case Irene's watching, but mostly I walk in the other direction, toward the boardwalk. Or I stay in and polish the peach-colored vases. That's the trick to keeping them shiny and glowing. Sometimes the phone rings and it's Peter, Irene's accountant husband, saying things like, "Penny wise, pound foolish," and begging me to go back to him. I've explained to him that I'm not Irene, and he seems to understand—says he even prefers it that way—but still he badgers me to change my mind. I often hang up on him, but it doesn't seem to offend him in the least. In fact I think he likes it. He always calls right back.

The calligraphied sand-dollar sign still hangs outside the window and rattles when the wind blows. The birds still come around, but I think Irene was wrong about them all along; I think it was always company they wanted, not food. Though I am not a bird person, I wave to them when I see them at the window.

The one change I've made is to throw out the lumpy futon and the floor pillows and replace them with a sofa, because I'm realistic enough to know that most middle-aged people feel foolish and uncomfortable sitting on the floor like teenagers, whether they admit it or not. The futon was an affectation on Irene's part, and a desperate one, unworthy of her. The sofa is pretty—white with pink and yellow flowers on it. I could afford to buy it. I can afford anything I want; every time I turn around, I'm saving eighty-five dollars an hour. But really, when you look at it, the help Irene gave me, the new haircut, the new town, the courage to break through the dog door of my life—that kind of help is beyond money, don't you think? You can't begin to put a price on it.

The Glass House

In the fall of 1969, my father had an affair—a serious one—with an artist named Molly Chu. This story is about them, but I find I can't keep myself out of it, can't help tracing back my own role in the affair. Because, after all, it would never have happened if it weren't for me.

In the summer of 1969, I had just turned eighteen, just graduated from high school, and was waiting for my life to begin.

I was a particularly young and naive eighteen. I think my father was both relieved and horrified by my naiveté. On one hand he was the doting father of an only daughter, an only child, and part of him must have wanted to keep me safe from the evils of the world. On the other hand, he didn't suffer fools gladly, and he must have been appalled by how little I knew. I didn't know how much a pound of hamburger cost. I wasn't exactly sure who'd been president before Eisenhower. I must have sounded ridiculous when I tried to argue with him over Vietnam, about which I knew absolutely nothing.

My mother had none of the mixed feelings about me that my father must have had. If she could have figured out a way to keep me home forever, safe, she would have done it. We lived in a beautiful house overlooking the ocean—in my memory it is all windows, nothing but polished glass. The house was my father's idea, his dream—the best of both worlds, he said, commuting to the bustle and vitality of the city during the day, driving back to the solitude of the ocean at night—but it was my mother who became addicted to the life there. She gave up her CPA job in Portland and started a small tax consulting business out of our house. It didn't amount to much—not that it mattered, my father made enough money that her income wasn't needed—and there were whole days, I think, when she didn't talk to anyone but me and my father, and once a week Mrs. Shekler who came to clean the house. She seemed perfectly happy with that arrangement—she worked a little, gardened, took walks on the beach, never seemed lonely—and I think she wished I could be happy with that sort of life too. She was disappointed that it wasn't enough for me.

Fortunately for my mother, there was a very good, small, private college just two hours from home, nestled in the hills above Portland. Astor College had once been a private mansion. Liberal (what college wasn't in those days?), but not too liberal, Astor was made to order for the sons and daughters of well-heeled, overprotective parents. It had acres of immaculately tended grounds, stained-glass windows in the library, a twelve-to-one student/faculty ratio, a rose garden, a goldfish pond with a fountain. It had everything except a moat around it, and it might as well have had that. Plus, one of its trustees was an old pal and client of my father's.

It wasn't hard to talk me into Astor. My father just called up his trustee pal and asked him to send a catalog. One look at those

glossy pictures of students reading Doris Lessing and James Bald-
win on the lawn, the rose garden in the background, and I was
hooked. I was timid as well as naive, and though I would never
have admitted it, two hours away was about as far as I was ready
to venture.

In midsummer the college sent preregistration forms, and I
promptly signed up for yoga, an upper-level English class on the
Bloomsbury group, an art class called "Form in Color," and
another one called "Chinese Brush Painting." It was a squirrelly,
chaotic time—requirements were being done away with right
and left, and there were no rules that prevented me from taking
this peculiar assortment of classes my first term instead of the
standard lineup of freshman comp and intro to psychology.

It was, in fact, my father who suggested I take the Chinese
brush-painting class. He was looking over my registration forms
one night after dinner, and spotted the class and the name of the
instructor—M. Chu. "Maureen," he said, calling my mother over.
"Look at this."

My mother, still in her gardening clothes with her hair tied
back in a ponytail, went to sit beside him on the sofa. They made
an oddly matched couple, I suppose, though I never thought of it
that way; I was used to seeing my mother in sweatshirts and
jeans, my father in starched shirts and navy-blue ties. My father
never seemed to feel the need to change out of his business
clothes at the end of a day, and he wore his pressed gray suits with
such natural elegance and grace that he looked as comfortable in
them as my mother did in her grubby garden clothes.

"Do you think M. Chu could be Molly Chu?" my father asked
my mother.

His passion—it was much more than a hobby—was contempo-
rary art. He collected it. It was an investment, he was always careful

to say—a kind of game, to see if he could pick up-and-coming artists and gamble on their work appreciating over the years. But I could see it was no game. I watched him sometimes in the evenings, after dinner, gazing intently at one of the paintings on the wall as though memorizing each line and brush stroke. He seemed as happy, as at peace, during those moments as I ever saw him.

"Wouldn't that be wonderful?" said my mother. "But can it be her? I thought she lived in San Francisco."

Earlier that year, while on a business trip to San Francisco, my father had gone to an art opening and been so taken with the work of an artist named Molly Chu that he'd bought one of her paintings as a present for my mother. It was a delicate watercolor of a tumbling wisteria vine, impressionistic and sensual, and it presently hung on a scroll above my parents' bed.

"She must be here on one of those one-term appointments," my father said. One of the things Astor prided itself on, and bragged about at some length in its catalog, was its commitment to the arts. Every quarter the college brought in a visiting artist, writer, or musician to teach a class, so the students would have the experience of working with someone famous, or sort of famous.

"I'm sure it's her," my father said. "How many painters named Chu can there be? What a wonderful opportunity, Jill," he said to me. "I met her in San Francisco at the opening when I bought her painting. She seems like a wonderful person, very warm, very bright."

I didn't argue. I loved the wisteria painting. I signed up for the class.

But, bad news. The college wrote back apologetically that the Chinese brush-painting class was full. It was a popular course, and upperclassmen had first choice.

"Let's not give up yet," my father said when the letter arrived. He picked up the phone, called his trustee pal who got his secretary to track down Molly Chu—for it was her, all right, and yes, it was a one-term appointment, and she was subletting an apartment in northwest Portland. The minute my father got her phone number, he dialed it, explained who he was, why he was calling. "My daughter's heartbroken. She loves your work. I wouldn't ordinarily ask for special favors, but it's her only chance to take the class. It'll be her first term at college, and it would be such a thrill for her. Yes . . . yes. That's generous of you. She'll work hard — I promise." He winked at me. "I would. I do. Yes, my business is in Portland. Maybe we could meet for lunch. I'd be interested in buying another of your paintings. My wife and I love the wisteria."

He hung up the phone. "Done," he said to me, and smiled.

◆

When the time came, it was my father who drove me to Astor, with my new typewriter, my towels and sheets, my new bulletin board to hang over my desk, my art supplies, my brand-new checkbook with $1,000 deposited into it, which was supposed to be more than enough to last me the whole term, and I was sure it would be. It seemed a vast amount. I had packed everything I could possibly imagine needing for the next three months. I was pretending that I was really leaving, that I was going much farther than two hours away. I planned not to return home until Christmas break.

My mother's excuse for not going along on this trip was that there wouldn't be room enough in the car for all my stuff if she went too.

At the time, I didn't know exactly what was wrong with my mother. I still don't, really, but I suspect some odd strain of agoraphobia. It wasn't that she was afraid to go out of the house; it was that she was afraid *for* the house. She was afraid it would burn down, that the neighbor would forget to feed the cat and he would starve, that someone would break in, if she left for a night. And she was getting worse; lately she hated to leave even for an afternoon. She'd get halfway out the driveway and go back, certain that she'd left the iron on, or the coffeepot, or the stove. She had Mrs. Shekler come in two days a week now instead of one, to do errands that involved leaving the house—grocery shopping, picking up dry cleaning.

She cried when she hugged me good-bye. My feelings weren't hurt that she wasn't coming. I knew she loved me. And besides, it was a treat to be with my father alone. It made the journey seem more momentous, somehow, that my handsome father in his pressed white shirt and tall military bearing was taking time out of his busy schedule to escort me to college.

As the car pulled out, I turned back to look at my mother. I carried away a mental picture of her, waving awkwardly—she was trying to wave and hold our cat Jack in her arms at the same time—the ocean in the background. She was smiling and crying, and Jack was struggling in her arms; he had his eye on some birds flocking in the ancient spruce tree in front of the house; he was dying to get down and get at them.

It was a rainy day, the roads slick, but my father took the winding road over the mountains as he always did, with confidence and grace, just slightly over the speed limit. I was never nervous when he was behind the wheel; I always felt safe with him. He made driving seem like an art, like ballet. Whereas my mother was a nervous driver—generally far too cautious but once in a while making some wild maneuver, an illegal left turn or a lane change without looking, that got her into trouble.

My father clearly enjoyed driving. He often drove to San Francisco on business when it would have been so much easier and faster to fly. And of course he drove into Portland every day to work. I think driving used up some of his nervous energy. He had his secretary, who had a rich melodious voice and some training as an actress, read poetry by Yeats, stories by Faulkner and Salinger and Fitzgerald, into a portable tape recorder, and he would listen to the tapes while he drove. When I learned that the poet Wallace Stevens was an insurance executive, I thought of my father. Not that he was an artist himself, but he appreciated creativity; he admired it, I now think, more than any other human quality.

"Write to us," he said to me when my things had been loaded out of the car and into my cell of a dorm room. Like my mother, he was going along with the fiction that I was leaving home, that I couldn't take the bus into Portland and be at his office in less than half an hour any time I wanted to. "I'll be waiting to hear how you like the Chinese painting class."

He hugged me hard and swiftly—too swiftly to give me a chance to get teary-eyed—and then he drove away in the rain. Fast, confident, lifting a hand for one final wave.

◆

Chinese brush painting was held on Thursday nights, in what had been the greenhouse when the college was a private mansion. It still smelled like a greenhouse—musky, earthy, faintly tropical.

Molly Chu wore her thick black hair in a shoulder-length pageboy. She had a round face and dark eyes, wore black pants and a long royal-blue silk shirt. Her hands were plump and dimpled and graceful, and she was already laying out her brushes and paper, mixing ink, when we arrived.

There were thirteen of us in the class. The limit had obviously been set at twelve, and I was the extra, the interloper, though no one knew that but Molly Chu and me. We sat at long tables, two per table to give us room to spread out our rolls of rice paper. But one table—not mine, as it turned out—had to make room for three.

She sat at the front, facing us, at a table all her own.

The first thing she did was to pass around a wallet-sized picture of her family—a daughter who looked to be about my age, a son maybe a year or two older, a husband. "My husband's name is Paul," she told us."My daughter's name is Marie. My son's name is James."

Her husband was not unattractive but certainly not striking—someone you wouldn't normally notice, and that's why I wonder now if I had some sort of premonition, because why else would I scrutinize so carefully the picture of someone I didn't know? And I did scrutinize him. I concentrated on him, not the children. I didn't give them a second glance, but even now I can see him, smiling uncomfortably into the camera.

But no, I had no premonition. It was just that what she did was so unusual, a college professor passing around pictures of her family.

I was obviously not the only one who thought so. I saw the other students giving each other sidelong amused, questioning looks. Molly went on. "I love living in San Francisco," she said. "I love the blend of cultures. My father is Chinese. My grandfather was a traditional Chinese calligrapher. He is the reason I became an artist. I worshiped my grandfather, and when he died, I cut off my hair—it was down to my waist then—to show the depth of my grief. My mother is American. I have a French grandmother. My daughter is named after her. And so my own art is a blend—mainly traditional Chinese, but with a little Monet and Cézanne as an influence. I am telling you these things so that you will get to know me quickly, because we do not have much time together and I want to teach you as much as I can. I have been painting since I was four years old. I can do a painting in a matter of seconds"—and she demonstrated, dipping a large brush into the ink and making a few deft strokes, black birds swooping across a white sky—"but I am not doing it in a few seconds, I am doing it in forty years plus a few seconds. Do you see? I cannot give you those years of experience, but I will give you what I can. We must use the time we have together wisely, and not waste it. Now we will begin."

She showed us how to mix water with the thick black ink to get varying shades of gray. Some artists, she said, used only black ink, but we would use three shades—a pure black, a medium gray, a light gray—so that we would get subtle gradations and a three-dimensional effect. Our paintings, of bamboo and chrysanthemums, water lilies and orchids, would look as though they were alive.

She had us come up in groups of four to watch her demonstrate how to hold the brush. It was nothing like the way you held an American watercolor or oil painting brush—you held it straight up, perpendicular to the paper, your fingers arranged in a complicated way around it, and when you painted you used your whole arm, never just the hand and wrist.

Right away, I saw that I had a problem. I was left-handed, and the procedure she was demonstrating was complicated enough that I could not seem to transpose it to my left hand. What should I do? I asked her.

"It will not be a problem," she said to me firmly. "Simply use your right hand. All traditional Chinese painters paint with their right hand. You will find that you have no trouble."

I was not remotely ambidextrous. I dipped my brush into the paint with my right hand, expecting awkward movements, a shaky line. But the line of ink looked more graceful than I would have thought. Molly made a few adjustments, straightened the brush, moved my fingers a fraction of an inch this way and that. "Again," she commanded. "Good," she said. "Good."

She had brought a record player, and she played Chinese music for us to paint by. We practiced painting bamboo leaves, over and over—loading the darkest ink onto the base of the brush, the lighter ink at the tip, starting with a firm pressure at the beginning of the stroke, then lightening up as we drew the brush along. We must practice over and over again, she said, to build our confidence. The best stroke was a quick, fluid, confident one—if you hesitated at all, you lost the momentum and the line was ruined.

She passed around tiny sesame-seed cookies for us to eat during our break, and then we were back to work again. From time to time she would turn down the music and talk to us—sometimes demonstrating a particular brush stroke, sometimes just talking in general about her life.

What all did she tell us during that first class? She spoke rapturously of nights spent staying up till dawn with friends, drinking green tea, playing music, arguing about art, *doing* art together. She didn't waste her time on passive activities like watching television, she told us. She talked as though she never slept and never needed sleep. The apartment she was subletting belonged to a friend who was on an extended trip to Portugal, and she had made it her own—bringing her favorite wind chimes with her from San Francisco, her special tea set, a spice jar to put flowers in. She carried these things with her always, even when she was going to spend only one night in a hotel. We should do this too, she told us, should always surround ourselves with objects we loved.

How did all these topics come up? How did they relate to each other? I have no idea. She told us that even when she was younger and hadn't had a lot of money, she always hired someone to clean her house, because housecleaning could be an art and it was better to pay someone to do something well than do it yourself in a mediocre way. No one can do everything well, she told us, and the best way to live was to concentrate on doing the things you liked and were good at.

At some point in the evening, the students who had been snickering and nudging each other stopped. We all of us fell under her spell; of course, I had been under it from the first moment.

At nine-thirty she clapped her hands and told us it was time to wash our brushes. The clapping of her hands startled me as though I'd been in a trance. That was when I looked out the windows of the greenhouse and realized how dark it was.

◆

Three weeks into the term, my roommate obliged me by having a nervous breakdown, or something, and dropping out of school. I hadn't liked her, had often wished her gone. I felt somewhat guilty after she left, as though I'd put a curse on her. But I was thrilled to have the room to myself. I remembered what Molly Chu had told us about making even a one-night hotel room your own and set about transforming my dorm room into a painting studio. I had thought the thousand dollars in my checking account would last forever, but without blinking I spent a hundred of it on a celadon vase. I spent more money on flowers to put in the vase—fresh chrysanthemums and orchids at least once a week. I moved the furniture around, putting my ex-roommate's desk against mine for a surface large enough to spread out my rolls of rice paper. I bought dozens of candles, so at night I could paint by candlelight instead of the harsh overhead light in the room.

Sometimes when I practiced, I had doubts. I had always gotten A's in art, always felt confident drawing or painting. I couldn't help thinking, now, that being forced to paint right-handed must be holding me back. If I could only use my left hand, I could paint so much more naturally. I did try it a couple of times, but I had come too far, practiced too long in class with my right hand; it seemed like starting at the beginning again, going back and relearning how to use the brush with my left hand. It didn't feel natural, as I had thought it would, but stilted and awkward. Also, I felt guilty. Molly wouldn't have approved. I decided she must know what she was talking about and went back to painting with my right hand.

♦

Soon after my roommate left for good, I got a call from my father. It was the first time I'd had a call from him. He and my mother were both faithfully preserving the illusion that I was away—we wrote dutiful weekly letters to each other.

He told me that on Wednesday he planned to stay overnight in the city—he did this occasionally, at the Edgeware Hotel, if he had an early breakfast meeting the next day. Would I like to meet him for dinner? I could take the bus into the city. He thought he might give Molly Chu a call to see if she could meet us, since he was still interested in buying another of her paintings.

I hung up the phone, elated. Dinner out with my father was always an occasion, and—I had to admit this—I was glad my mother was not coming along. My mother had very little interest in food—she just didn't see the point. And of course, going out to eat meant being away from home. When we went out for dinner, she would usually order something she thought the cat would like, and then take most of it home for him. Throughout the meal she'd be restless, always looking at her watch.

But my father delighted in the experience of dining out. Though he was a moderate, self-contained man who never drank more than a cocktail or two before dinner, never drank more than one cup of coffee in the morning, and rarely ate a second helping,

at elegant restaurants he became expansive and generous, order-
ing appetizers and elaborate desserts.

On such evenings, his nervous energy in check, he would eat
slowly, appreciatively, as though he had all the time in the world,
the evening spread out before him like a beautiful fan. He enjoyed
the attention of the waiters and liked to talk to them. On such
nights he was not preoccupied, the way he often was at other
times; he would lean toward you, rapt, interested, and charmed by
everything you said.

So you can imagine what this night was like for me—my
glamorous father whisking me away from the dreariness of dorm
food, into the city for a candlelit feast, a table by the window overlooking the glittering lights. And the added pearl: my glamorous
teacher, who had no idea of the hours I spent practicing my painting, practicing to be like her.

Their affair began that night. Molly told me that, later. It wasn't
planned to happen. They were both innocent. The evening had
been orchestrated, all right, but not for that purpose. My father
invited Molly for my sake. He knew how the world worked; he
knew the value of personal connections and knew I would be too
shy to establish them. He wanted the class to be special for me,
and he was afraid that, left to my own devices, I would sit in the
back of the room and Molly Chu might not notice me at all—and
the whole experience would be wasted, as though I were watching
it from the window of a train passing by.

Molly arrived at the restaurant ten minutes late, in a flurry of
apologies and laughter. "I'm sorry," she said. "It's always harder to
get a taxi in the rain—why is that? And there's something going
on at the Coliseum, some sports thing." She waved her hand dismissively to indicate the unimportance of sports things. My
father, who had no use either for sports, smiled. "I had to wait *for-*

ever for a taxi." But she didn't seem in the least put out. She wore a black, shiny raincoat that crackled when she took it off to reveal a silk dress in the royal blue she favored. She smelled like an exotic tropical flower.

She slid beside me in the semicircular booth, so that I was in the middle. She entered immediately into the spirit, my father's spirit, of the evening. He had ordered a dry martini, and she said, "Oh yes. I'll have one too." When it arrived, she ate the olive first, with relish, popping it whole into her mouth. "You know, I'm not a drinker. Not at all. But martinis are so festive. Who can resist the *idea* of a perfect martini?"

She was not merely following my father's lead, matching her mood to his. She was that sort of person herself; she liked a festive evening. I knew that about her already. I thought of the snacks she brought to class, the rice cakes and sesame cookies and steamed buns, and the way she presented them to us with such enthusiasm, making the eating of them a ritual. (I thought disdainfully, disloyally, of my mother, who sometimes forgot to eat entirely.) And I thought about the other evenings Molly'd told us about in class, those evenings when she'd stay up all night long with her artist friends, drinking tea and playing music. She had told us so much. I felt as if I knew her intimately, knew everything about her life. It didn't occur to me to wonder what her husband did on those party nights, whether he was with her. She hadn't mentioned him since the first night when she passed his picture around.

We ordered tiny bluepoint oysters as an appetizer. "No cocktail sauce," my father warned me when they arrived. "Just a squeeze of lemon to bring out the flavor." I nodded. I had never eaten raw oysters before. I loved them immediately. They tasted and smelled like the essence of the sea. (I have been back to the Edgeware Hotel several times since that night, and it seems in recent years to have become a ghost of itself, the restaurant no more than a glorified coffeeshop, no oysters on the menu anywhere.)

"Jill is wonderful," Molly said as we ate our oysters. She sipped her martini, patted my hand. "My best student."

"I'm not surprised," my father said, and smiled at me. "She does everything well."

Basking in their approval and attention, I became suddenly brave, confessional. "I worry," I said to Molly, "about the fact that I'm left-handed. I'm afraid because of that I can never be really good. I want to be really good. I would like to be"—I had never said the words aloud—"an artist."

"Don't worry about it at all," she said firmly. "You can be every bit as good as if you were naturally right-handed." Of course, how would she know, being naturally right-handed herself? She'd never had to struggle with it. But I didn't think of that then. "What is important," she said, "is that you concentrate fully, that you have the *chi*, the life force, flowing through you as you paint. And you do have that. I can see it when I watch you."

The end of the evening stole up on me, the way it did on Thursday nights in class, like the end of a delicious dream. I saw my father push away his plate. I glanced at my watch and was amazed to find that it was after ten. We had been at the table for more than four hours. But it wasn't over yet.

There was chocolate mousse for dessert. At Molly's urging we ordered three instead of one to share, as my father and I would have done if we'd been alone. She was not as naturally moderate as my father, I noticed. She ate more than he did, and with even more pleasure. She ate bread, slathered it with butter. Only now, looking back, does it occur to me that she ate a little greedily.

At the end there was coffee (I was struggling to acquire a taste for it), and a special surprise—the waiter brought three snifters of marc, on the house. He set my snifter down before me without a blink. My father didn't blink either. Maybe he'd forgotten for a moment who I was exactly. Maybe I had fooled him, and myself, into thinking I had transformed into some older, more sophisticated version of myself.

Though my parents often had a cocktail hour before dinner, I was as innocent about alcohol as I was about everything else. I'd had a beer or two urged on me by high school boyfriends, but on those occasions I'd only pretended to drink. I'd never been drunk, never even tipsy, in my life. So it didn't take much. I sipped the warm golden liquid in that snifter and the world turned rosy and slightly out of focus. I even giggled, embarrassingly, but softly enough that nobody seemed to notice.

It had to have been obvious that night that something was happening between Molly Chu and my father. Any fool could have seen it—I can see it when I replay the evening in my mind. I didn't see it then.

It was still raining when we went outside. My father hailed a taxi for me. My memory is that, though it was a busy night—that sports thing just letting out at the Coliseum, and lots of disgruntled umbrellaed people on the sidewalk, peering in vain for a cab—my father lifted a hand and a taxi materialized out of thin air. He gave me twenty dollars for the fare, hugged me good-bye in that swift hard way he had.

And then, of course, he and Molly must have turned to each other . . . and that was the moment. They went up to his hotel room or to her apartment—I don't know which. Molly told me a lot, later, but she didn't deal in such specific details, and though I was hungry for them I was too shy to ask. One place or another, though, they spent the night together.

◆

The dinner, which my father had planned so carefully for my benefit, did have its intended effect—Molly did single me out for extra attention from that night on. I became the one she asked to help her pack up her brushes and paper, the one she walked out with after class. The other students began eyeing me jealously, but I didn't care. I could feel it—she was beginning to treat me as her friend instead of her student.

I've never felt again the way I felt that term. Evenings, days, weeks seemed to float by without my being conscious of time passing. I stayed up all night, often, painting by candlelight. I don't know if what I was experiencing was what Molly had in mind when she talked about the *chi*, the life force, flowing through us while we painted. I do know that it sometimes seemed as if I painted in a waking dream.

Between painting, yoga, and reading *To the Lighthouse*, I was as whacked-out as if I'd been experimenting with seven different kinds of drugs—which I never did. I knew my classmates were doing drugs—all I had to do was walk past other dorm rooms and smell the pot and patchouli wafting out at all hours of the day and night. Not me. I was oblivious to all of that.

In the distant background, the war went on. At Astor, we were all against Vietnam, but we protested the war not by bombing buildings or demonstrating, but by holding candlelight vigils around the goldfish pond. We petitioned the dining hall to serve nothing but plain rice and tea one night at dinner—to what practical end I have no idea. It wasn't as if the college planned to send the money it had saved on our one dinner to the troops in Vietnam. It was the concept of sacrifice that appealed to us, I guess. Most people went out for hamburgers afterward.

My other art class, "Form in Color," fell by the wayside fairly early on. The bright acrylics the teacher used seemed jarring and garish after Molly's class. In Chinese painting class, Molly told us we weren't nearly ready for color yet. It would take months, maybe years, to master the art of those subtle variations of grays and blacks.

I still went faithfully to yoga, but the Bloomsburies faltered sometime in mid-November. Even Virginia Woolf's considerable charms could not compete with Molly Chu's. So I would be getting an Incomplete in that class. But I wasn't too worried about my less-than-stellar first-term performance. My father, I was sure, would understand, and that was all that mattered.

I was getting to be good at Chinese painting. I would have been supremely untalented not to have developed at least some measure of skill, considering all the hours of practice I put in. I'd developed enough confidence that I'd dared to do a painting—in black and those subtle gradations of gray that Molly prized—of the ancient spruce tree in front of our house, which I planned to have mounted on a scroll as a Christmas present for my parents. I had asked Molly's advice about this; my parents had never been the sort of parents to hang their daughter's finger paintings on the refrigerator door, and it seemed presumptuous to give them a painting of my own when they had a collection of work by real artists worth thousands of dollars. If I gave my parents a painting, it had to be a good one, a real painting.

"It is a fine painting," she said firmly. "The best you've done. He will love it." She amended her statement. "They will love it."

As the term came to an end, I felt something magical, irretrievable, slipping away. I could not take Molly Chu's class again—she would be going back to San Francisco. I might never see her again.

◆

When I went home for Christmas break, I left my brushes, my rice paper, my ink block, in the dorm room, also my tea set and the celadon vase. I remember feeling very ambivalent about this decision—but in the end I was afraid, somehow, that if I didn't leave these traces, these artifacts, of myself behind, the dorm room would no longer belong to me, and I would come back to find it as stripped and bare as it had been the day I moved in.

On a more practical level, there'd been mention of my being assigned a new roommate the following term, and I had some vague notion that if the dorm director came in and saw how completely I had overtaken the room and made it mine, she would realize how much it meant to me and would let me keep it all to myself. (This was, of course, another of my naive notions. I was indeed assigned a new roommate at the beginning of the next quarter, and no one—including my new roommate—was shy about telling me to move my stuff, pronto, back over to my side of the room. But that was later.)

At first when I went home it seemed that nothing much had changed, except that my mother seemed to have grown more obsessively attached to Jack, the cat. Also, the scrolled wisteria painting had moved from its place above my parents' bed and was rolled up and standing in a corner of my father's study, but this didn't seem especially unusual. Artwork in our house was often in transition, older pieces making room for new.

The storm arrived on the Saturday before Christmas.

There was nothing, at first, to indicate that it would be anything other than a normal winter storm. The ocean was dark and roiling, the wind blowing fiercely, the rain blasting down, but I was used to that. It probably ought to have occurred to me that, even with the wind and rain, it was unnaturally dark for midafternoon, but somehow it didn't. It must not have occurred to my parents either, because nobody moved to turn on any extra lights.

My mother and I were sitting at the dining table, putting

together a jigsaw puzzle. Or rather, trying to put it together. The problem wasn't only the dim light. The other problem was, we had no idea how many pieces might be missing. My mother had quirky habits concerning money. She would often decide to buy something—an oriental rug, a sofa, a coffee table—without even asking the price, but then she would turn miserly when it came to small things. The jigsaw puzzles were in this category—she had found a flea market that regularly sold used ones for fifty cents, and one of Mrs. Shekler's duties on errand day was to go there and see what bargains she could pick up.

This particular puzzle was a cloying, sentimental picture of puppies and kittens in a basket, roses in the background.

My father was pacing the house like a caged animal. I know the reason for his mood, now. I didn't then, but I think it must have scared me a little, subconsciously, the way the unnatural darkness in the afternoon must have scared me without my quite realizing something was wrong. For all his nervous energy, my father was never bored, almost never irritable. He always brought work home, even on holidays, and he was happy being at home, working in his study, or gazing at his paintings or out at the ocean. But now he didn't seem to have any work to do; he didn't seem to have anything to do. He wore a thin gray sweater and khaki pants, and he looked uncomfortable in them. He poured himself a drink, which I'd never, ever, seen him do this early in the day. I glanced at my mother, but she was absorbed in the jigsaw puzzle.

The jigsaw puzzle clearly irritated him. The ugliness, the overblown sentimentality of the picture, must have offended his sense of taste. Not to mention what a complete waste of time it was.

But from my point of view the puzzle was not a total waste of time. While we worked together on the puzzles, my mother and I were able to converse after a fashion. She had cried and hugged me when I arrived home, but after she stopped crying she didn't seem able to think of anything to say to me. We had always had our troubles communicating, but it seemed to me she was even more distant and distracted than usual. I would come upon her idly flipping through magazines or staring off into space. Her cooking, which had never been especially good, became disastrous. She served us steaks cooked to leather, baked potatoes cold and hard in the middle. I had begun to miss dorm food. It was only when she was working on our puzzles that she seemed focused, that she seemed really in the room.

"I'm looking for a completely black piece," she said now. "Sort of like a flower shape. See here? For the dog's nose."

I searched, but didn't find one. "Maybe it's missing."

"Oh, I hope not. It will spoil the whole picture if it is."

My father gave a snort of disgust.

I remember that clearly, his snort of disgust, a split second before the storm hit in earnest. Rain smashed against the windows. The two dim lights we'd had on flickered and went out, and suddenly it was dark—as dark as seven or eight o'clock at night. The wind blew harder.

I remember my mother's face across the table, shadowy. My father, standing by the window looking out at the sea, was just a dark shape; I couldn't see his features at all.

The cat was the first to realize what was happening. He'd been dozing on the sofa, and he suddenly leaped onto the coffee table, sending an expensive crystal figurine spinning across the table and onto the floor, smashing into a million pieces.

"Goddamnit!" my father, who never swore, shouted.

Jack's eyes were wild, his fur electric, his tail puffed out fat. My mother, so attuned to the cat's moods, realized then too, and cried out harshly, "Graham! Get away from the window."

Even then, I wasn't afraid. I'd seen plenty of rough weather over the years. Living as we did on this isolated stretch of coastline, the winter storms offered just about the only excitement there was to be had. I would watch them from our picture windows, feeling the same thrill, the same sense of pleasurable fear, that I got from watching a horror movie.

And, of course, I wasn't afraid because my father wasn't afraid.

"For God's sake, Maureen," he said. "It's nothing. Just a storm."

"Please," she said, and he sighed and stepped away from the window—more, I'm sure, to forestall any hysterics than because he thought there was any danger.

"Calm down," he said. "We'll listen and see if there's a weather report on the radio." But he'd forgotten; the power was out.

I went to my bedroom and searched for the old transistor I'd gotten for my thirteenth birthday. I couldn't remember having turned it on in years. Its batteries, though weak, amazingly still worked. We leaned close to the radio—it was hardly bigger than a pack of cards—and listened for a weather report. The battery was just about dead when a wheezy announcer's voice came on and said, "A special report. Residents of the northern coast from Twin Rocks to Arch Cape are advised to take extreme precautions. Gale winds expected over the next twenty-four hours up to eighty miles an hour. Mud slides have been reported."

"You see?" said my mother.

"Extreme precautions," said my father. He took a calm, deliberate sip of his drink. "We're taking extreme precautions. We've got some candles, right? We'll just stay inside where it's safe and wait out the storm."

There was the crackle of static, and then, just before the battery went dead for good, the announcer's voice came on again, barely more than a whisper. "Residents of homes west of Highway 101 are advised to evacuate. We repeat—"

My mother looked up at my father. We were both waiting for him to tell us what to do, but he didn't say anything.

I thought of his driving skills, his perfect confidence behind the wheel. "Daddy," I said—I hadn't called him that since I was ten—"why don't we drive into Portland? Stay the night at the Edgeware till the storm blows over." I thought, we could eat oysters, drink marc. We could be safe.

My father didn't answer at once, and I thought he was considering my idea. But then he said, firmly, "There's nothing to worry about. We're not going to panic over nothing."

Another blast of wind and rain shook the windows. *People who live in glass houses*, I remember thinking, but the saying didn't fit.

"Graham," my mother said. "Please."

And then I thought, *the eye of the hurricane*, because that's what it felt like—the house a dark square of silence, the wind and rain swirling and shrieking outside. "All right," my father said finally. "Get your coats and get in the car. I'll be right behind you."

"What do you mean?" my mother asked. "Why aren't you coming now?"

He spoke calmly. "I just want to check on a few things, make sure all the windows are shut tight so there won't be any water damage. And I might bring out some of the artwork."

"Graham—"

"Just in case. The paintings are irreplaceable, Maureen." He repeated the word. "Irreplaceable. Besides, there's nothing to worry about. This is just a precaution. Get in the car. Jill," he said when I didn't move. "Do it. I'll be right along. I promise."

I got our coats, and a blanket to wrap Jack in. I remember that

I felt sorrier for Jack than anyone. He was so terrified of riding in the car.

We waited there in the cold car, my mother and I, Jack in his blanket. The wind rocked the car, and the rain crashed down so hard it felt like someone hurling heavy rocks down from the sky and onto the roof. My father, getting soaked to the skin—he hadn't bothered to put on a coat—brought out in total three armloads of paintings, till the trunk was full, and he had to put some in the back seat with me. When he tried to go back again a fourth time, my mother grabbed his arm and cried, "No!" He leaned in then, patted her hand, and said, "I'll be right back. Stay here. I just want to check to make sure the deck posts are holding firm."

The rest is a jumble I try not to think about. There are the sounds of splintering wood, breaking glass, but I have to strain to hear these sounds because the sounds of wind and rain are so much louder. All of it happening so quickly there's no time to think, to make a decision. My mother stayed in the car, holding Jack, and I stayed there too. We stayed because he had told us to. It was only at the very last second that I pushed open the car door—the wind fighting to slam it shut again—and got out. By then it was too late.

When it was all over, I saw that the ancient spruce tree by the front door had been ripped out of the ground and was lying flat, its tangle of roots exposed like (this is the way my father would have thought) a giant piece of abstract sculpture. It may have been the spruce tree that killed him. It may have been the house itself—a falling beam, a brick, a pane of heavy glass. That was Molly's theory—it was the house itself that killed him—but how can anyone know for sure? It was hours before they could get in and extricate his body from the rubble of wood and glass—what was left of the house. The rest of it had slid down the cliff into the sea.

♦

You could say Molly shouldn't have told me anything at all—and maybe she shouldn't have. But who else was she going to talk to about him? I didn't blame her. And besides, isn't it better for me to know the truth instead of being left, always, to wonder?

She knocked on the door of my dorm room one day during the winter term, sometime in February. Fortunately my new roommate was away for the weekend. I didn't like this roommate any more than I'd liked the first one. If my father had been alive, he would have made a phone call, would have found some way to get me back my single room, my art studio.

I almost didn't recognize her. She had cut her hair.

And then I knew—the last, the missing, piece of the jigsaw puzzle, the picture finally making sense. Molly said, "You understand, don't you, why I couldn't go to your father's funeral," and I nodded.

I invited her in. She was wearing her crackly black raincoat, a black dress underneath. I even brewed some green tea on my little hot plate, to be hospitable. We sat side by side on my narrow dorm bed.

My father had broken off his affair with her the week before the storm hit, Molly told me. "He had tried to leave your mother. He had told her he was in love with me, that he wanted a divorce. She said he could have his divorce, but that she would fight to keep the house."

Apparently—amazingly—my father had not anticipated this, had not expected that my mother would defy him in this particular way. What had he been thinking of? Had he really thought that she would give in, go away so quietly, that he could have Molly and his perfect dream house too? But maybe he did think that. My father, always, was a man used to getting what he wanted.

My mother's insistence on keeping the house changed everything, Molly said.

"I told him, let her have it. Let her keep it. Let her keep every-thing. My God, Graham, I said. We can work. We're both hard workers. We can start over, and in a few years we'll have a house you'll love more than this one."

She would have left her own husband in a minute. She wouldn't have cared where they lived. She could live anywhere, so long as she had a flat surface to paint on, so long as she could have her wind chimes and a jar of chrysanthemums on the table.

They had talked all night long. She'd cried—not weak, plead-ing tears, she told me, but angry tears. She knew she could make him happy; there was no doubt in her mind of the course they should take, and she was furious with him that he couldn't or wouldn't see it.

In the end, they left things unresolved. He asked her to give him some time, a week or two. He would talk to my mother again. Molly was leaving anyway, for shows in Los Angeles and San Diego. She said she would talk to him when she got back.

But then in L.A. she heard a brief news flash about the storm in the Pacific Northwest. No details were given, but "I knew then and there what had happened," she said. "I knew at that moment he was dead."

I wasn't sure whether to believe that last part or not—it sounded false and overdramatic. But what did it matter whether she'd had some psychic connection with my father at the moment of his death? He was dead, all the same.

"But I know what his decision was," Molly said. "He chose the house over me. He chose the house over his own happiness. It's clear what he was doing. He was trying to save the house. And in the end, the house killed him."

That too sounded melodramatic. But I think she was proba-bly right that his final decision had been to leave her. For one thing, her wisteria painting was not among the ones my father had tried to save. I can't help wondering if he would have tried to save my painting if he had known it existed, but he didn't know. It was rolled up—Molly had helped me mount it onto the scroll—under my bed, tied with a Christmas ribbon.

◆

I stayed friends with Molly over the years—first in a furtive, secretive way out of deference to my mother, then later, when it didn't seem to matter, openly. Who else could I talk to about him, besides Molly? We are friends to this day, all these years later, at least she would say that, does say that, though we do nothing anymore beyond exchanging Christmas cards. "To my dearest friend Jill," she writes on them, and signs them, "Always, Molly." She has stayed married to Paul. He's a genuinely nice man—I went to visit him and Molly once, years ago, in San Francisco, and he greeted me graciously, as though he didn't know whose daughter I was. For all I know, Molly still passes his picture around to her students on the first night of class. She still teaches now and then, though she is past seventy.

I kept painting off and on during the rest of my freshman year, practicing at my cramped dorm room desk. Without the class and Molly's strong-willed presence, without her looking over my shoulder, I gave myself permission to begin painting with my left hand. It didn't work, though. I kept feeling ambivalent, guilty. And besides, how could I be sure that her praise of my work hadn't always been, at its heart, a way to get to him? I lost confidence; my brush began to falter in midstroke. Finally I gave it up altogether, though I still have the brushes and the ink, the leftover roll of rice paper. I keep them in that boring, ordinary way of people who take up hobbies and then abandon them, always vowing to get back to them "someday."

I still have nightmares about that winter storm, but in day-light I try never to think about it. I do think, sometimes, of that night at the Edgeware Hotel when I ate oysters for the first time and drank marc, when I imagined myself sophisticated, older than my years, poised on the threshold of a glamorous adult world. I think of my father, conjuring a taxi out of thin air on a busy rainy night, and I wonder how I could ever have been that innocent.

Pretty Night

Pounding bass and shrieking guitar and fifteen-year-old boys trying their best to look depraved—that's the band. It's impossible to make conversation over the noise, but Will doesn't know anybody to talk to anyway.

His daughter Emmy stands in a corner in her new short haircut and her new starflower-print Laura Ashley dress. She and her girlfriends are pretending to have a great time, cupping hands to each others' ears, shouting secrets over the music, laughing, but they're not fooling anybody. The looks they give the dancers are sideways, desperate glances, full of longing.

Will is working on his third glass of orange-Hi-C-and-ginger-ale. It has taken him awhile to realize that the punch is bright orange on purpose, color-coordinated to match the sagging loops of orange-and-black crepe paper which hang everywhere. School colors.

Marcia would never refuse a request from Emmy's school, and Will is wishing, not for the first time, that his wife didn't suffer from such a relentless sense of parental concern. He's fairly sure nobody else's parents got suckered into this. He recognizes the school principal, and there are three or four other adults who look so excruciatingly bored they can only be teachers who've drunk this same punch over and over, who never in a million years would have signed that contract if they'd realized dance duty was an unwritten requirement of the job.

He can't be angry with Marcia, though—she tries so earnestly, always, to do the right thing. He is glad for her sake that she caught that cold at the last minute and therefore is not here tonight to blame herself for the fact that Emmy, Laura Ashley dress or no Laura Ashley dress, has not been asked to dance even once.

◆

Though she has been too polite to say so, he knows Emmy doesn't want him here. On the way to the dance, she sat silent in the car's front seat with the flattened-down air of a cat on its way to the veterinarian, while her three friends, Jana and Beth and Megan, giggled nervously in the back seat. When they arrived, Will pulled up in front of the gym and said, "Why don't you girls get out here, and I'll go find a parking space?" and Emmy said softly, "Thanks, Dad," and only then did it dawn on him how much she must have dreaded walking into the dance with her father. Maybe she had even lost sleep over it, the moment of embarrassment looming large in her mind for days the way such things do when you are fourteen years old. Will remembers such moments from his own childhood, petty fears and insecurities growing giant-sized, out of all perspective. "Mountains out of molehills," his mother used to mock. Will never, ever, will say that to Emmy; however, he undoubtedly says things just as cruel—as unaware as his mother with her jokes about imaginary mountains. He will never know the ways in which he hurts her. Emmy, always so polite, will never tell him.

He stands in a corner, feeling like a traitor. Except for his being here, witnessing it all, Emmy would be able to go home and answer Marcia's questions with bright white lies: "I had a great time . . . everybody liked my dress . . . of course I danced."

♦

The band is in high gear. It slides from one number to another with barely a pause—or maybe it's all one nightmarish, endless piece. Suddenly—the relief he feels is palpable—he sees Emmy being led out onto the dance floor.

The boy leading her is so average looking, so sandy-haired and utterly forgettable, that Will has no choice but to stare at him, knowing he'll never recognize him again without concentrating this moment on his features. The kid is wearing sneakers and a jacket over a T-shirt. He'll get taller eventually—he hasn't grown into his hands and feet—but for now, Will can see Emmy slouching, as unobtrusive as possible, dancing down to his level.

Will wants Emmy somehow to spring to life on the dance floor, to surprise her partner and everybody else with her grace and rhythm. But she looks, next to the boy, as average and gawky as he, and a little chunky besides, though that is the dress's fault and not hers. The two of them merge into the writhing crowd so completely that for a moment Will can't make out which girl is his own daughter. They all seem to be wearing the same kind of oversized cotton-print dresses, and he wonders what has prompted these girls to want to look like dowdy prairie housewives.

He remembers the day Emmy and Marcia brought the dress home, how excited Emmy was about it, modeling it for him as though it were white satin instead of plain navy cotton. "Don't you like it, Dad?" she'd asked, a tiny pleading note in her voice, uncharacteristically concerned about his good opinion. So he said,

"Sure," in a phony-hearty voice, with Marcia standing by anxiously. Then Emmy came closer and showed him the magic of the dress: the pattern of white starflowers sprinkled over the dark blue background. The flowers were as complex as snowflakes, so delicate you had to look closely to see them at all.

From this far away Emmy's dress looks plain, drab navy blue. Her dance partner is close enough to see those starflowers, but Will has a feeling the kid is not attuned to such subtleties. He finds himself resenting the boy, though he ought to be grateful to him. Now Emmy won't have to lie. When Marcia says, "Who asked you to dance?", Emmy will have a real person to describe.

Will reminds himself that this dance of Emmy's is private, that he doesn't belong here—and to remove himself from the temptation of spying on her, he goes in search of another drink.

At the punch bowl, a fight has broken out between two boys. The principal, with a world-weary air, breaks it up singlehandedly. By the time order is restored and Will has refilled his glass, the song is over and the band at long last has decided to take a break. Someone turns up the gym lights—a big mistake. Now everybody has a jaundiced look. The murky darkness was better.

On his way back to his corner, Will spies Emmy's sandy-haired dance partner talking to another boy. Both are surreptitiously lighting up cigarettes. This is the kind of behavior Will, as chaperon, is supposed to call a halt to, but he doesn't want to blow his cover. He edges closer; the boys don't notice him. Now, in the light, he can see the sprinkling of acne on the sandy-haired boy's neck, can read the lettering—"COBRA"—on his T-shirt. The boy takes a drag on his cigarette, blows it out slow, and says, "Jesus, what a pack of dogs!"

The cold drink in Will's hand makes him shudder.

They stand there snickering.

Will searches the crowd for Emmy. She is easy to spot this time, conspicuous in her misery. She's too far away, he's almost certain, to have heard the boys' words, but they're looking at her and the nature of their laughter is unmistakable.

He steps closer, and the boys notice him for the first time. They smile at him, all innocence. They're practiced; the cigarettes in their hands have dematerialized.

There is nothing he can do. He'd like to punch the kid, who comes barely to his shoulder. He wants to strangle him. He has never felt so powerless. The boys slide away from him, and a few minutes later, just as the band is starting up again, Will sees them head out the gym door. Though he keeps his eyes on the door for the rest of the evening, they never reappear.

Emmy does not get asked to dance again. In the end it is her friend Jana who rescues them all, plucking at Will's sleeve, pale, saying, "Please, Mr. Lawrence, do you think we could go home soon? I don't feel so good."

"I'll get the car and meet you outside in five minutes," he says. "Three minutes."

It's a clear night, full of stars, and as Will walks to the car, he remembers a dance from his own adolescence. It was a magical spring night like this one, so intoxicating that everyone spilled out onto the lawn, music following them through the open windows, Japanese lanterns glowing. Even as he thinks of it, though, the memory fades, eluding him. He suspects it never really happened like that. He wishes there were some way to tell Emmy that memory will soften this night too, that someday she won't even remember what some little jerk of a kid thought of her.

They are all dead quiet on the way home, no nervous giggles from the back seat. Will drops them off one by one, Jana, Megan, Beth, waits till they are safe inside with the door locked before driving away. When at last he is alone with Emmy, there is nothing to say. They are in this together, silent conspirators, and when they get home and Marcia asks brightly, "How was the dance?", both of them will lie.

There is only one thing he can think of to give her. Though they are only a few blocks from home, Will pulls the car over to the curb and gets out. He walks around to Emmy's side and opens her door. "Come on," he says, and holds out his hand. "I want you to see something."

"Oh, *Dad*," Emmy says, and he feels a little hopeful, because her voice carries a trace of that half-exasperated tone she often uses when things are normal. And after a minute of hesitation, Emmy does take the hand he offers and lets him pull her to her feet. The touch of her hand is stronger, more confident, than he expected.

"It's a pretty night," he tells her. "Look."

He had thought he might need something extraordinary—a shower of shooting stars, a comet, even an airplane they could pretend to believe was a UFO—but it isn't necessary. "I just wanted you to see what a pretty night it is," he says, and Emmy nods. It's enough, this ordinary starry night in their own quiet neighborhood. Will puts his arm around his daughter's shoulders, and they stand there together for a moment before going home.

The Fat Dancer

Martin Cunningham, six-foot, lanky, part-time accountant, flutist for the Pacific Heights Chamber Music Society, is dead. Hit by a car six weeks ago, and I know how it happened as sure as if I'd been standing there. Walking home after music practice, flute tucked under his arm, Martin would have been looking up at the stars instead of where he was going.

Pacific Heights at ten o'clock at night is sleepy and safe: soft-lit street lamps, tiny English daisies glowing against clipped lawns. No need to pay attention, no reason to suspect a fast car would come shooting out of nowhere. I'll bet he never knew what hit him. His head so full of music.

In my more hopeful moments, I used to think, if Martin could feel one passion, why not two? I was optimistic to the end. Well, almost to the end.

◆

Martin told me, fairly early on, that he was looking for a "permanent, part-time" relationship.

"It sounds like a want ad for a typist," I said. Martin looked hurt, and I felt guilty. I knew perfectly well he didn't like to be teased. I also knew that for Martin to be asking for my hand in a permanent part-time relationship was the equivalent of any other man threatening to throw himself off the Golden Gate Bridge if I didn't elope with him. But it wasn't enough for me.

"It's not that I don't love you, Elizabeth," Martin used to explain to me, sadly. "It's just that I don't have the temperament to sustain an intense relationship over the long term. I know that from experience. And besides, music takes up so much of my time."

This was true. Monday night was Martin's flute lesson, Tuesday night was his ear-training class, Wednesday night the Chamber Music Society rehearsed. Thursday night, for fun, he played clarinet with a little jazz combo at a sedate bar on Sacramento Street. Friday night the Chamber Music Society usually had a performance. The rest of the week Martin practiced his flute at home and worked on people's taxes. That left only Saturday night for me, because on Sunday night Martin liked to stay home by himself and listen to *Mystery Theatre* on the radio. He needed a night apart, he said, without music or numbers or people. It balanced things, set things in order. That was the way he explained it to me.

◆

When Martin was alive, this was my idea of a perfect day:

Take a Thursday, in early spring. I'd get up at five-thirty and practice my *pliés* and *rélevés* in the middle of the kitchen floor, while the cat ate her breakfast under the table. I have one of the few landlords left in San Francisco who will let you have a cat, and for that reason I will stay in this apartment forever.

Next I'd take the bus to work, getting off two stops early so I could walk along the marina and watch the boats, the bright-colored reflections they made on the water. I have to be at work early. I work in the flower department at Cost Plus Imports on Fisherman's Wharf; the flower delivery truck arrives at seven, and I have to be there to meet it. I don't mind. I take a two-hour lunch to make up for it. The flower job is the best job I've ever had.

Our flowers are good flowers, fresh-picked, no chemicals added. They smell the way flowers are supposed to. They're not too expensive, either, and I like that. I like selling a bunch of red tulips, for instance, to a secretary on her way to work. I like to imagine her riding up in the elevator, her arms full of flowers. Or, if somebody wants to buy just one flower, I understand that. I'll wrap up a fifty-cent carnation as carefully as a big bouquet. I realize that one flower can lift your spirits as much as a dozen.

After a day of selling daffodils and hyacinths, I'd ride the bus home (carrying all the leftover flowers that couldn't be kept over) and make a dinner of, say, fresh pasta with parmesan cheese, which I'd eat at my very own butcher-block kitchen table. I always wanted such a table, and I bought it for next to nothing from Cost Plus—fifteen percent employee discount, another thirty percent off because of the crack in one leg, which nobody has ever noticed.

While I ate, I'd look down from my second-story window onto my neighbor's garden. It's a tiny garden, a city garden. It contains, among other things, one artichoke plant. My neighbor is an elderly Chinese lady who sometimes stays out after dusk, weeding and hoeing. If she sees me watching her from my window, she will often wave.

After dinner, as the perfect end to my perfect day, I'd walk over to Sacramento Street and drink a glass of wine and listen to Martin play the clarinet.

Martin never thought he had much feeling for jazz. It's true he was no Benny Goodman, but what I liked was the fact that he relaxed a little when he played jazz. The Chamber Music Society was a surly group, with clipped haircuts (even the women) and calluses on their fingers. I used to go to their performances, but afterward, if I dared to compliment them, one was sure to snap, "Are you kidding? We were hopeless. I *ruined* the solo." Martin was never surly, but I think the self-critical attitude of the group rubbed off on him and made him nervous. I stayed away from him on chamber music nights, but I loved to hear him play jazz.

He played clarinet till midnight or later, but I had to leave after the first set so I could get up for work the next morning. Martin would walk me home, briskly, since his break was only twenty minutes long. There was time for just one good-night kiss at my doorstep. Sometimes it was a sweet kiss, sometimes an abstracted kiss if Martin's mind was still on his music; sometimes it was even a semi-passionate kiss. Thursday was, now that I think about it, my favorite night of the week. It was even better than Saturday, because there was still Saturday to look forward to.

Although I wanted more from Martin, it seems to me now that the life I had with him was as perfect as I could have wished for— and that the wistfulness, the moment of longing I felt when he kissed me good night at my doorstep, gave my life a certain edge that made it richer. Sometimes the promise of passion is more exciting than the fulfillment of passion.

Now and then I tried to talk to Martin about that longing, and I think he knew what I meant, though I can't be sure because he always translated everything into musical terms. He talked about the "ambivalence of dissonance." He said, "Take 'The Rite of Spring,' for example. The human mind strives for harmony, yet a

musical piece is often more challenging—though less satisfying—
if that harmony is not supplied."

I like to think that Martin and I understood each other.

♦

Today was a Thursday, in early spring. Six weeks and one day
since Martin died.

I got up even earlier than usual, and after my twenty minutes
of *pliés* and *relevés* and pirouettes, I did some more complicated
steps. I'm trying to master the *grand jêté*, a leap in which you are
suspended briefly in midair. In that instant, I hope to understand
what it feels like to fly.

My teacher, Mrs. Glover, cautions us against practicing complicated steps on our own. Practicing a step wrong can cause
untold harm, can set you back months. Patience is the key, she
says. Like Martin, Mrs. Glover believes in the mastery of technique; but I am impatient. I want to fly, and I can't wait until every
Saturday morning, from nine to ten-thirty, to learn how to do it
right.

Originally, I began taking ballet for other reasons. I was too fat,
for one thing. I went on a lot of diets, but one of the endearing and
frustrating things about Martin was that he loved me no matter
what I looked like. Five pounds, even ten, one way or another—he
didn't notice. I asked Martin once if he dreamed in music, the way
people who study a language intensively sometimes begin to
dream in French or Spanish. He said yes, he supposed he did,
which supported my theory that Martin operated on a plane that
had very little to do with the physical or the visual. Something
about me, for example, perhaps translated into a Beethoven sonata
in Martin's mind; perhaps he didn't see me at all. Once I cut five
inches off my hair; he didn't realize.

So I thought maybe something less obvious than diets and lipstick would get through to him. I thought the ballet lessons would make me feel beautiful, graceful, sexy, *inside*, and that inner confidence would make me less inhibited. No longer ashamed of my body, I could allow myself total freedom and abandon—and then maybe my own abandon would release Martin's inhibitions and we could experience, together, unbridled passion for the first time in either of our lives. Passion was the main thing, I'd decided.

That was more or less what I had in mind with the ballet lessons, and that was why I practiced so faithfully. I did my *pliés* and *relevés* and five pirouettes as though they were necessary steps in a witch's spell. If I did them every day, without fail, one morning I would awake and everything would have changed. If you gather the damiana leaves by the light of a new moon and sleep with them under your pillow every night until the next new moon, you will win the heart of your lover.

Of course, the dangerous part of this experiment was that I might discover Martin had been right all along. He usually was right. He may have loved me as much as he could. There may have been no further ardors lurking within him besides his music. In which case it would become necessary to find someone else with whom to experience unbridled passion.

That was the conclusion I had just about come to when Martin stepped off that curb into the path of a speeding car.

◆

A lawyerish-looking man with graying temples has been stopping to buy flowers from me every couple of weeks, for as long as I've been working here. Early afternoon, around two o'clock, he walks by, swinging his calfskin briefcase. He buys a dozen roses, usually. Pink ones.

At first, I speculated that they were for his secretary (a gentle motherly lady who'd been with the firm for twenty years) or his wife (a stylish but sweet-faced woman who'd been his childhood sweetheart and with whom he was still madly in love). He *could* have been on his way to an afternoon tryst with his mistress, but if so, I didn't want to know.

One day he ordered his usual dozen roses, and after I'd wrapped them up and he'd paid me, he handed the roses back and said, "Today I bought them for you."

A few weeks later, he asked me for a date.

That's the kind of thing that began to happen after I started taking ballet lessons from Mrs. Glover. It really did work. I felt prettier, more graceful, and it showed. Even the flower-delivery-truck man asked me out to lunch. It worked on everybody except Martin.

◆

It was raining today when I woke up. I practiced my ballet as usual, and later leaped onto the bus with the same momentum I'd use to push off into a *grand jêté*. I got off the bus two stops early, to walk past the marina. On rainy mornings, the boats look as if they've been painted in watercolors. Plus, it's nice to go for a little walk right after my ballet practice. My steps feel lighter, more buoyant, then. I like wearing those billowy float dresses from Pakistan ($15.95 at Cost Plus, less fifteen percent employee discount, less an additional ten percent Manager's Special Spring Fever Discount). It feels as if a gust of wind could lift up my dress like a balloon, like a parachute, and I'd never come down again.

Before starting ballet, I never felt anything remotely like that.

I think, in somewhat the same way, Martin was at his best, musically, right after his practice sessions. That's why I can't feel too sad about the way he died. It seems a terrible thing to say, but Martin would probably never have been a great musician; he was too concerned with technique. (They all were—that was the Chamber Music Society's biggest problem.) He wouldn't let himself reach beyond. It seems to me that the nearest he got to greatness were those nights walking home after practice, floating, reaching for stars, letting himself transcend. That's what I like to think, anyway.

◆

Once at work I decided to set up the flowers outside, just as usual. I put up the umbrellas to protect them. I like working outside, even in the rain. Indoors just isn't the same; it's more like an ordinary job. Besides, flowers smell fresher in rain.

Martin's funeral was in Sacramento, where his parents live. I rented a car and drove up, feeling like an intruder. I'd never met his parents.

"I love you as much as I could ever love anyone," Martin used to say to me, sadly. His declarations of love were so careful, so excruciatingly honest, so qualified. He didn't want to mislead me; he didn't want me to expect too much from him.

He kept me at arm's length, and so now, never having loved him wholly, I don't know how to grieve for him. I could go, tomorrow night, and listen to the Pacific Heights Chamber Music Society perform, minus Martin, at the Unitarian Church. I could sit in the back pew and weep unobtrusively. I could rent another car and drive to Sacramento this weekend to put flowers on his grave. But that, especially, is something I don't want to do. At Cost Plus, I always liked the fact that we never made up expensive arrangements for weddings and funerals. I always felt that people bought our flowers because they saw the stand and suddenly decided flowers would be a good thing to have—that no one bought flowers from us because of occasions, or obligations, or penance.

◆

Five days before Martin died, I told him, over our Saturday night dinner of tortellini at a little place on Fillmore Street, that the lawyerish-looking man had asked me for a date.

"I said no," I told Martin quickly when I saw the look on his face. Then, because it was, after all, an issue that had kept me up the whole night before, I pressed on. "But part of me—just a little part—wanted to say yes."

"Why?" asked Martin. He had put down his fork. When Martin was at all upset over something, he was physically unable to eat. It accounted for his thinness, I think. He worried so much before every performance, jazz or classical, that he couldn't eat.

"Because he said he thought I was ethereally beautiful. He said I was ethereally beautiful and that buying flowers from me brightened his day." Martin didn't say anything; he looked bewildered. "I know," I said. "I know it's a corny line. It's an incredibly corny line. But it worked. It made me feel ethereally beautiful to have someone say the words. Do you know what I mean?"

"You are beautiful, Elizabeth," Martin said sadly. "Do you think I don't love you?" And then he was quiet for the rest of the evening. He hardly touched his tortellini. Whereas I, just as nervous, ate all of mine and some of his besides.

I hope our Saturday night conversation was not what Martin was thinking about when he stepped off that curb. I hope he was thinking about music and transcendence, maybe even about passion.

Looking back, I think I had known for a long time that I was going to leave Martin, that the ballet lessons were a kind of preparation for leaving.

◆

People bought more flowers today—because of the rain? Probably because of the rain. It makes sense to me. A gloomy, gray day; you pass a patch of daffodils; you buy some to give you the illusion of sunshine.

I watched the flowers dwindle. At this rate there wouldn't be any left over to take home, and I felt sad about that. I didn't have much to look forward to after work. No jazz music. Now, no flowers. No Chinese lady watering her garden—the rain would take care of that.

The Chinese lady's company wasn't very satisfying lately, anyway. Before, I found it nice that our lives touched in such small ways—there was a momentary warmth in our chance meetings, in the way we waved at each other through window glass. It was the same warmth I got when a customer stopped for a moment to talk, didn't just pay his money and hurry on. Now, those small encounters with strangers were all I had.

A stranger, telling me I was beautiful. It seemed a hollow thing.

The lawyer arrived at four-thirty, just as I was lowering the umbrellas. I hadn't seen him coming; if I had I would have fled. I hadn't spoken to him since Martin's death. Whenever I saw him coming, I ducked inside, collared another customer, or took a break if I could. He had no idea Martin had died. Only the flower-delivery-truck man knew that. None of my customers knew Martin had even existed.

"You do a good business," the lawyer said, smiling. "So busy I never get to talk to you anymore. No roses left?"

"Nothing left," I said. "It's been a good day."

"Too bad. What excuse can I have for talking to you, taking up your time, unless I can buy flowers from you?" He had such a jaunty way of swinging his briefcase. It might have been full of rose petals or confetti instead of legal briefs.

The careless way he swung that briefcase made me think of Martin. I remembered the way Martin used to carry his flute case, so protectively, under his arm, as though it were something fragile and utterly irreplaceable. I'll bet he was clutching it like that even at the moment he realized a car was coming at him.

I stopped short, my hand on the umbrella, and Martin came into focus, in all his intensity. I could see him standing there, tucking his flute case under his arm, so carefully, and all the feelings came back—the irritation, the anger, the frustration—and the love I had for him in spite of it all. I felt the beginning of tears I hadn't been able to cry for the past six weeks.

The lawyer was saying something. He looked filmy through my tears, like a picture taken under water.

"What about those?" he was asking, pointing to one lone bunch of daffodils sagging in the corner. "If they're all that's left, I'll take them."

"I'm sorry," I said. "You're too late. They're already promised to someone else."

He raised an eyebrow. "Are you sure?" he said. "Are you sure it's not a promise you could break?"

"It's an absolutely unbreakable promise," I said.

He shrugged. "Another day, maybe." He smiled and walked away, jauntily, swinging his briefcase—on to the next flower stand, perhaps.

I paid full price for the daffodils even though they were wilted. The rule was you could only take home, for free, flowers that were left over at the end of the day, flowers nobody else wanted. I paid for them, and I wrapped them in pink tissue paper, because even flowers that are slightly wilted can lift your spirits, especially if you weren't expecting any at all.

♦

Later in the evening when I took the daffodils over to the bar on Sacramento Street, the bartender let me put them on the piano. He gave me a wine carafe to use as a vase. I had arrived early, and only the bass player was there tuning up.

"No," he said when I asked him. "We've tried other people, but nobody's worked out. Martin never thought he had much talent on the clarinet, but he underestimated himself. We miss him. We've decided we won't replace him for a while."

The drummer arrived, and then the pianist.

"Will you play 'Solitude'?" I asked them. "Will you play 'Memories of You' and 'I'm Getting Sentimental Over You'?"

"Sure," said the bass player.

"Will you play 'Dedicated to You' and 'All Alone' and 'You'd Be So Nice To Come Home To'?"

"We'll play anything you want us to play, Elizabeth," said the piano player.

"Will you play 'Remember' and 'That Certain Feeling' and 'After You're Gone' and 'The Way It Might Have Been'?"

I stayed until long past ten. Nobody heard the clarinet but me. I walked home in the rain, but it wasn't a cold rain—it was a spring rain smelling of flowers. I walked carefully, so as not to let the memory of Martin's music slip away. When I got to my doorstep I leaped into the air, weightless for one split second, lifted.

The Things We Find

Darla and I case joints the way burglars do. No—better than
burglars. We're more thorough. Of course, we're looking for different things, not tangible things like stereos and TV sets and
jewelry. Darla and I look for secrets.

We've found a few. The best one so far is Mrs. Thurston's
mink coats. She owns two. One hangs in the front hall closet and
one hangs in her bedroom closet, way in the back, and as far as I
can tell, they're identical. My theory is that Mrs. Thurston's husband bought her one coat, and her lover bought her the other, and
her husband is so unobservant he hasn't even noticed the second
one. Darla says, why don't you take it one step further? Suppose
Mrs. Thurston has *two* lovers, and she tells her husband she
bought both coats on her secretary's salary. It could be true; Mrs.
Thurston seems brazen enough that it could be true.

In general, though, people have fewer secrets than you might
imagine. Or maybe, as Darla says, they just destroy the evidence.

Of all the people we've baby-sat for, we haven't found a single diary or secret drug stash, and the closest we've come to a dirty photograph was a picture of Mrs. Helm sunbathing on the beach with her top off. She was lying on her stomach, though, so you couldn't see anything, and she didn't look sexy so much as embarrassed to be caught off-guard like that. We haven't found any illicit love letters; all we ever seem to find are tacky Hallmark cards that say, "To My Darling Husband on Our Anniversary." Half the time these aren't even hidden away; they're right on the mantel for anybody to read, which is *really* tacky.

We are becoming disillusioned.

But we have high hopes for tonight. Tonight we are baby-sitting for the eight-month-old baby of Paul Kazman and his second wife, Maura.

My parents don't give parties the way they used to—it's probably been three years since they gave a party—but when they did, I remember Paul Kazman would come with his first wife, Marilyn. I thought she looked like Cleopatra, although I realize now that was just because of all the eye makeup she wore. I was only twelve or thirteen at the time, and not much interested in my parents' friends. But even then, Paul Kazman was hard to ignore.

He was—is—gorgeous, in a way that has Darla panting with lust but only makes me nervous. I never know what to say to beautiful men. I'd say Paul Kazman's most attractive feature is his thinness, which only heightens the perfection of his bone structure. He looks gaunt, tortured, romantic.

Maura Kazman is romantic too, but in a determined, sort of desperately feminine way. Tonight, for example, she wears a satin blouse buttoned up to her chin, and a cameo brooch, and a black velvet calf-length skirt. That might be all right, barely, but then she overdoes the effect by wearing her hair up in ringlets. *And* she has on white lace stockings. That's desperate.

Paul Kazman teaches sociology at Keaton Hill College, and Darla's older sister, who takes "Sociological Perspectives" from him, says that he is hot, which is hardly big news. All you have to do is look at him to know that. Darla's sister says that if she had a dollar for every student Paul Kazman has had an affair with in his teaching career, she could fly to Rio and back. Darla's sister says she heard it was especially bad right after his divorce—that he just went wild—but now he's settled down and is trying to be faithful, trying to make this second marriage work.

We have already decided we don't like the present Mrs. Kazman.

"Are you sure you've had experience with babies?" she asks us—and she tells us about ten times where to reach them in case something goes wrong, and what temperature the baby's formula is supposed to be. For a while, it seems she's going to change her mind and not go out at all. She acts very suspicious. You can tell she's convinced we're going to neglect that baby.

Well, we do neglect him a little. We sort of forget about him. The minute they are out the door, Darla says, "Where shall we start?"

I vote for the bedroom, anxious to inspect Mrs. Kazman's underwear. Wouldn't it be great if under that fluffy-romantic exterior, Maura Kazman wore some truly indecent underwear. That is *the* only justification I can see for dressing like Meg in *Little Women*. Darla says she doesn't think Mrs. Kazman is the type, but there has to be some reason why Paul married her.

It turns out, though, that Darla is right.

"Look at this, Jen," says Darla, going through drawers. "Yech. J.C. Penney. White cotton."

"*Dingy* white cotton," I say. "Stretched out, dingy white cotton. I can't believe it."

"Thirty-six A," says Darla. "That's the worst size to be. Built like a football player around the shoulders, and you have no cleavage whatsoever. No wonder she wears her blouses buttoned up to here."

We find no satin sheets; we find no books on tantric sex. Of course the absence of those things is significant. They've been married less than two years, after all. Still, we are disappointed.

"Well, we'll come back to the bedroom later," says Darla. "Let's go on to the study. Paul Kazman is a word person, after all. I say his secrets are likely to be written down."

Paul Kazman's study is sexier, by far, than the bedroom. Soft and muted lamps—too dark to read by, but romantic—circle the room. The smells of pipe smoke and leather and old books tickle my nose. In one corner is a rolltop desk (with, there must be, a secret drawer) full of scraps of paper and envelopes poking out of pigeonholes. "Look," I say to Darla, pointing out several of these envelopes addressed to Paul alone, with no return address.

"Significant," says Darla.

On top of this rolltop desk is a picture of Maura Kazman wearing a sun hat and standing in front of a rose garden. The picture seems forced and dutiful to me, like the little family-picture cube my father keeps on his desk at work.

What is far more interesting is the picture of Paul himself, standing with his arms around a pretty, dark-eyed girl of about fourteen and a blond boy of eleven or twelve. They all look happy. They are laughing. The picture seems spontaneous, not posed at all. I stare at it.

"Of course," I say. "His other family. His children by Marilyn."

"Wow," breathes Darla reverently. "Who do you suppose took that photograph? It looks like a recent one, doesn't it? Do you suppose the ex-wife herself took it? My sister says that when they were studying marriage as an institution, Paul told the whole class that his ex-wife is one of his best friends. That they're better friends now than they ever were when they were married. Do you believe that? I'll bet he still wants Marilyn, and that's why he's chosen a second wife with a similar name. I'll bet you anything that if they're pretending to be friends, it's because they still have a thing for each other."

Darla looks up from the picture. The dim and romantic light shadows her face. "Tell me again, Jen," she says in a whisper. "Was she *really* that beautiful?"

I have already told Darla, several times since we learned we were going to baby-sit here tonight, that I honestly can't remember what the first Mrs. Kazman looked like. It was a long time ago, those parties of my parents, and all I really noticed was the eye shadow. But now I say, "Yes. She was stunning. She was the most beautiful woman I've ever seen."

Darla sighs. "I knew it," she says.

We go through Paul's desk systematically, but we find no secret drawers. We don't even find where a secret drawer ought to be. What seemed so promising yields nothing in the end. We find lecture notes—pages and pages of lecture notes on sociological perspectives and the nuclear family. "*Bor*-ing," says Darla. We find a plumber's bill, a car insurance statement, an invitation to speak at the Knife-and-Fork Club.

"Here we go," says Darla finally, breathlessly. "It's from her." She holds it out, a sheet of thick, cream-colored stationery. How like Marilyn to have such stationery—sensuous stationery.

But Darla is disappointed. "'Paul,'" she reads, "'We need to talk about Jon and Amanda's college fund. My lawyer is tied up till the 26th. What about a lunch meeting the week after?' *Bor*-ing," says Darla. "Finances and child support. I can't believe there's nothing else."

"Maybe he's destroyed the evidence?"

Darla brightens.

I'm not especially concerned with what the letter *says*, but with the signature—"Marilyn"—written in a fragile hand I would never associate with this Cleopatra-like woman. It's like looking at a ghost's handwriting; maybe she feels like one, seeing her husband with that new wife and a whole new family. It gives me a chill. She *had* to have taken that photograph. I can see her standing there, wistful, focusing that camera, wishing with all her heart that things were the way they used to be.

"You know what we ought to do," I say. "We ought to create a little evidence. Leave a note, stuffed casually in one of those cubbyholes. Something Paul, or Maura, might not come across for months."

Darla would not have expected this from me, so she just stares. Usually she's the one to come up with daring ideas.

We consider one another for a long minute, and then start to laugh. "*Jen*," says Darla, but she can hardly get the words out, she's laughing so hard, "that would be a terrible thing to do!"

"No, no. You've got me all wrong," I say, waving my hands. "I'm not talking about some tacky note that says, 'Meet me at Motel 6, Room 205, Love, Gloria.' I'm talking about something subtle. Like, 'Dear Professor Kazman, Yesterday was the best yet. Love, Sarah.' I mean, she could be talking about yesterday's lecture, right?"

"Right," says Darla.

Darla writes the note; she has the more sophisticated handwriting. It looks very authentic. Looking at that note, with its bold slanting handwriting, the dramatic flourish on the "S" of "Sarah," I can see that girl in my mind's eye: the beautiful one with the sun-streaked hair who sits in the front row by the window, the one who has read all the theories, the one who dares to argue with him—but he likes that; he likes that spark of defiance. The electricity between them energizes the whole class.

We fold the note into quarters, then unfold it, then refold it and unfold it a couple of times, until it could be weeks old, or months old, or even years old. It might, for instance, have been written in that wild time after Paul's divorce, before he even met Maura—when he was on the rebound and trying, unsuccessfully, to forget Marilyn.

We stuff the note deep into a pigeonhole, and stand away. You can hardly see it—one small corner just peeks out.

There is no cause to worry. Nobody's going to find the note anyway, except possibly Paul, and he'll throw it away. If Maura finds the note, it means she's spying on him and doesn't trust him, and therefore she deserves whatever she gets. It won't be our fault.

"Well," says Darla.

And then we remember the baby.

We heat the formula to exactly the right temperature. It's important to get it right, to prove to Maura Kazman that we are responsible. It takes us almost half an hour of turning the heat on the stove up and down. In the meantime, Ford, the baby—a ridiculous name for a baby, and it has to have been Maura Kazman's idea—gets crankier and crankier and finally breaks into a howl. Ford's face gets as red and scrunched up as a withered apple. He screams until I think he will explode.

"Great," says Darla. "Just great." Finally we feed Ford his bottle, and he sucks on it and calms down.

"It's a miracle," says Darla. "Maybe there's Valium in that stuff."

While I stand holding Ford and his bottle, Darla looks through the refrigerator and the freezer and every one of the cupboards. "I can't believe it," she says. "There's nothing to eat in here." She's not exaggerating. There are six whole frozen chickens in the freezer. In the refrigerator are apples and eggs and formula and milk, and some potatoes that are so old the insides have pulled away from the skins, making them rattle when you shake them. The cupboards hold All-Bran and Shredded Wheat and whole wheat fettuccine.

"Every place I've ever been to," I say, "*every* place, they've had potato chips and Coke and stuff like that. And they've said, 'Help yourself to anything in the refrigerator.' Mrs. Thurston leaves white chocolates."

"It's part of the job," says Darla. "It's expected." We stand before the open refrigerator, me holding the baby. "I'm starving," says Darla.

"Don't you think this is significant?" I ask Darla. I go on about how the lack of any kind of real food in the house implies a lack of sensuality in their relationship. But Darla isn't as interested in this as she might otherwise be. "I'm *hungry*," she says. Darla gets peevish when she's hungry.

Finally, in the cupboard, behind the Shredded Wheat, we find a box of tapioca and decide to make pudding. This involves heating up milk again, and more messing around with the stove temperature. "How *bor*-ing," I say. The pudding turns out terrible, and we end up throwing it down the sink. Then we put Ford to bed, first debating whether to change his diapers, but he seems pretty calm the way he is. We decide to leave well enough alone.

We don't talk about the note. Neither of us suggests going back to the bedroom, or the study, or snooping in the medicine cabinet. Instead we go in the living room and turn on their VCR. We put on some old Goldie Hawn movie. It's just as well, because the Kazmans come home early, and there we are watching Goldie Hawn like it's what we've been doing all evening, in between heating Ford's formula and changing his diapers.

"It's not even eleven o'clock," says Darla when the key rattles in the lock. They walk in, and obviously something's wrong. They've had a fight. Maura's cheeks are burning; she looks as red as Ford in mid-tantrum. It doesn't take a genius to tell she's been crying.

But she puts on an act for us, saying, "Did you have a good time? Did you find a movie you liked? Oh, Goldie Hawn, good. Do you like Goldie Hawn?" She doesn't ask about the baby at first, though we can tell she's dying to. And when she does ask about him, she does it tactfully. "Did the baby give you any trouble?" she puts it, and that's nice, I think. It lets us off the hook. It suggests that if anything did go wrong, it was the baby's fault.

She doesn't have to put on this normal act for our benefit—we're only baby sitters after all, what's it matter what we think?—and I like her for it. My mother does the same thing. She always tries to pretend that she and my father haven't been fighting when it's perfectly obvious to anyone that they have.

Maura edges toward the hall, pretend-casual. "I guess I'll just go check on the baby, then," she says, and that's the last we see of her.

Paul doesn't even wait until Maura is out of earshot. "What a night," he says, leaning toward us conspiratorially. He's a little drunk. "All the fun was over by ten o'clock. *Miserable* party," he says, making "miserable" sound like a synonym for decadent.

That's part of his charm—that's why his students fall in love with him, this jaded manner, this way he has of taking you into his confidence, pulling you just for a moment into his wicked adult world. But I'm not so sure I want to be let in.

A glance at Darla tells me we're both thinking the same thing. It was a miserable party because Maura caught him necking with the hostess in the guest bedroom, probably. My mind whirls with the image of a darkened guest room, fur coats piled on the bed, the scent of the cold night air still clinging to them. I think of Paul and the hostess clutching each other, falling onto the bed, into those fur coats, stealing one passionate kiss and then another and another, knowing at any moment they could be caught. Darla looks back at me. We're on the same wavelength, all right.

"*Miserable* party," Paul says again, and winks at us. "I should have stayed home with you two and watched the movie." He's drunk enough that I think we shouldn't let him drive us home, and I should call my parents. But I'd be too embarrassed to do that.

We put on our coats and gather up our schoolbooks (which we always take baby-sitting—we never crack them, but they make us look reliable), and then, just before we leave, I pretend to have left one of my books in the study. Darla gives me a look—part "You coward!" and part relief. When it comes right down to it, Darla and I aren't cut out to be burglars. There's more to it than that, though—I no longer like the idea of Maura being hurt by our note.

In the study, it takes about ten seconds to retrieve the note and shove it deep into my coat pocket. Now if Paul and Maura Kazman's marriage falls apart, Darla and I won't have to feel in the least bit responsible.

I hope Paul Kazman will drop me off first, but no such luck. When he pulls up in front of Darla's house, she hisses in my ear before getting out of the car, "Call me first thing in the morning and tell me everything that happens."

Of course nothing happens, except that I ride in silence for twelve blocks with Paul. (I count the blocks.) Or rather, I'm silent. Paul hums along with the radio, absent-mindedly, off-key. He doesn't seem to mind my not talking. He acts preoccupied, and I wonder if he's thinking about leaving Maura.

I steal sideways looks at him, at his silver-flecked hair, his hollow cheeks and strong jaw, the deep lines around his mouth. And I think, he may be handsome but he's old. He's too old to have a new wife and a new baby, even if that baby does have an old-sounding name. But there is Maura, and there is Ford, and if Paul left them he could never go back to Marilyn and his other family, because you can't go back to the way things used to be. I know that, and no matter how hard I try (and I do try), I can't imagine any alternatives to Paul Kazman's life that don't depress me.

We drive down my safe, familiar street. He turns into my driveway.

"Good night, Jennifer," he says cheerily, just as though everything were normal, as though everything were fine. I hear him humming along with the radio as I shut the car door.

♦

My mother is waiting up in the kitchen, as usual. When she first started doing that, it annoyed me, but now I realize her waiting up doesn't have much to do with worrying about me or not trusting me, or anything like that. It just gives her something to do. She says she has trouble sleeping. My father, on the other hand, goes to bed earlier and earlier, it seems. I'll come home from the library at nine o'clock, and he'll already be in bed.

She's playing solitaire at the kitchen table and drinking coffee. I'm sure my father's in bed by now. I don't even ask about him.

"No wonder you can't sleep," I tell her. "Why don't you drink hot milk or something?"

"I know," she says.

"Or herb tea."

"I know." She sighs and slaps a red jack down on a black queen. She's wearing a faded pink robe that I just hate. I liked it when it was new—however long ago that was. My father bought it for her one Christmas, and I remember thinking I had never seen anything so beautiful, so shimmering and so glorious to touch. She gave up sending it to the cleaners a long time ago—

she just throws it in the washing machine. You can't even tell it used to be satin, it's so faded. I wish my father would buy her a new one. I'd like to buy her one myself—I have enough baby-sitting money—but things are pretty bad when your teenage daughter has to be the one to buy you a sexy robe.

Well, things are pretty bad.

"Did you have a good time?" my mother asks. I sit down beside her and nudge her to put the red seven on the black eight. No wonder she always loses. She doesn't concentrate.

"We were baby-sitting. How good a time can you have baby-sitting?"

"Oh, I don't know. I thought you and Darla used to enjoy baby-sitting."

"Yeah," I say. "We used to."

I decide to stay up with her tonight and pour myself a cup of coffee, get out some crackers and cheese. I know she hasn't eaten. "Black two on red three," I say, sitting down beside her again.

How normal, even cozy, a scene like this would appear to an outsider: concerned mom waiting up for her daughter, dad safe and sound asleep upstairs. If someone came to our house to spy, they wouldn't find any evidence at all. Oh, they might, if they were as alert as Darla and I, notice my mother's faded satin robe and that well-worn pack of cards and draw some conclusions, but they wouldn't be able to prove anything.

We stay up late, my mother and I, playing this game, keeping our secrets.

Phil's Third Eye

Phil's doing his laundry. He hates doing laundry so much that he puts it off till he doesn't even have *dirty* clothes left to wear— just stuff *beyond* dirty, so disgusting he can't wait any longer. Usually, like today, this happens on a Friday, right before a party. It's not exactly the greatest ploy in the world to try to meet girls wearing a week-old T-shirt. So he shoves everything into his laundry bag, and it won't all fit and he leaves a trail of socks and jockey shorts from his car to the Laundromat door. There's something creepy about washing your underwear in front of a room full of strangers. That's just one of the things Phil hates about laundry.

But he's got his copy of *Women in Love*, which he has to have read by Monday anyway for the test, so he might as well do it in the Laundromat as anyplace else. He's got his yellow pen, ready to highlight important-sounding lines for easy reference. It's always a good ploy, quoting from the text, and he's amazed how few people have caught on to it. Earns you extra points just like that. You don't have to *read* a book—you skim it, pick up the gist, quote a few lines, make it sound like you loved that book so much you've memorized your favorite parts. Phil's got the knack down. He's got a C+, maybe even a B going in this class, and he's achieved it without reading a single required book all the way through.

He's got his two Hershey bars, and after he feeds quarters into the washer and gets the clothes going, he feeds some more change into the Coke machine. Cokes and Hershey bars—that's another of Phil's secrets to success. His roommate Zeke swears by quart bottles of Schlitz, which is stupid. Phil's always telling Zeke, "You might as well take sleeping pills. The combination of some boring book and all that beer—you know it'll put you to sleep inside twenty minutes." Which it does. Zeke's flunking out. Just a matter of time before it happens.

Phil settles in. It's cold outside—that weird time in the semester after Thanksgiving but before Christmas break, when all anybody wants is to head off for skiing, be done with it. The air inside the Laundromat is steamy and stale, and he shrugs off his jacket. At least the place isn't crowded, only some big frumpy-looking woman in a housedress over in a corner, shaking what looks like a whole entire box of Tide into her machine—and a zoned-out druggie in a ponytail standing in front of a dryer, watching his clothes flap around. The druggie looks *interested*, for God's sake—he looks like he's watching a game show on TV, like he thinks something unexpected's going to happen inside that dryer any minute now. Phil hates those zoned-out hippie types. He just hopes the guy isn't going to come around and ask him for money. He hunkers down over *Women in Love* to make it plain that he's doing something important and doesn't want to be disturbed. You never know when guys like that are going to come around and ask you if you've been saved. Once one of them asked Phil if he was aware of his third eye, and if he wasn't, the hippie would be happy to show him how to find it.

The hippie had told Phil it was bad luck to wear his Dodgers cap, because the bill was obscuring his third eye. Creepy.

He flips through *Women in Love*. He highlights "There always seemed an interval, a strange split between what she seemed to feel and experience, and what she actually said and thought." Perfect. Next he highlights "A flicker of excitement danced on Gerald's face." That'll be good too—he can do some stuff about dancing as a symbol. He searches for another line with the word "dance" in it, but can't find any. That's okay. He can *say* there are all these references to dancing, and just quote that one line as proof. He flips some more. He highlights a few more lines at random. He's starting to feel the book coming together in his mind. He glances up. The druggie, still watching his dryer, is bouncing up and down on the balls of his feet, his own private dance. The guy's obviously hopped up on something—Phil doesn't know what, doesn't care. Twenty-year-old acid, probably. *Rotten* twenty-year-old acid.

In the background, the fat woman in the housedress is swigging coffee out of a red thermos, not even bothering to pour it into a cup, and studying the Laundromat bulletin board—those tacked-up notices advertising baby-sitting services or looking for a roommate or trying to sell some junker car for $75. Who would ever call some number off a Laundromat bulletin board to find a roommate or buy a car? Just the thought of it gives Phil the creeps. But that's probably exactly how that woman finds not only her cars and her roommates, but everything else in her life too. Pathetic.

He flips to the back of *Women in Love* to the Biographical Information part. First he highlights D.H. Lawrence's dates, 1885–1930, so he can work that in—show he knows historical context. He highlights "Lawrence's mother was a frustrated schoolteacher whose fierce ambition for her son pushed him to struggle toward a more intellectual life." Women in love, frustrated mother. There ought to be a connection there that he can work in. It's always important to talk about the title.

He glances outside now and then. The sky's turning bleak and white, looking more than ever like snow. Zeke wants to take off for the mountains first thing tomorrow if the Colorado snow report is good, says he can't stand to wait for Christmas break. Zeke wants to go now for a three-day weekend, drive back Monday, which would mean missing the *Women in Love* test. Zeke doesn't care about that, of course, but Phil's not sure what to do. He'll probably go. It's not a big deal. He can make up a good excuse and offer to take the test first thing Tuesday.

Except that money is a problem. They'll take Zeke's car, and Zeke will pay for all the gas, but still. He hates to keep borrowing money from Zeke. He shrugs. He'll figure something out.

Finally Phil's washer changes gears, shifts into its spin cycle. Great! Almost done. The machine bounces and vibrates like it's about to explode. Maybe he stuffed it too full. Should've split it into two loads maybe. Oh, well. Doesn't matter.

He's finished off the Hershey bars, and his hands are sticky. Better wash them before he goes to get his clothes out. There's a rest room in back, but getting to it means walking past the druggie, who's still standing in front of his dryer and staring at it, even though the dryer has stopped. Well, the key is to steer clear when he walks by, not to make any eye contact. If the druggie hasn't noticed his clothes aren't moving anymore, he probably won't notice Phil either. It'll be okay.

In the bathroom, he stands and looks down at his shoes. They're getting pretty disgusting. Most guys he knows just throw away their running shoes when they start to get disgusting. *Can* you wash running shoes? Phil has no idea. Anyway, it doesn't matter. He's not about to sit through another wash cycle just for shoes. Maybe he could buy new laces. At least that would help.

He washes the chocolate off his hands. Above the bathroom mirror is a fluorescent light about to die—he can tell by the high-pitched hum it's making, like some trapped insect.

Zeke is always teasing Phil that Phil's incapable of passing a mirror without looking into it. Well, not this mirror. The yellow walls of the bathroom and the dying fluorescent light make his skin look gray and pale. He almost doesn't recognize himself, and he looks away immediately. He doesn't even stop to comb his hair. Why would he? There's nobody in this place he's exactly looking to impress. He clicks off the light even before he opens the bathroom door.

When he comes out of the bathroom, everything happens so fast that he can't take it all in.

The fat woman in the housedress is standing right outside the bathroom door, staring straight at him, wild-eyed. The way she's standing, tensed up and still as a statue, it comes to him: she *followed* him over here, and she's been standing outside the bathroom waiting for him to come out.

She's holding a chair out in front of her, lion-tamer fashion. Her hair's all matted down and stringy. Sweat glistens on her forehead. She's breathing hard and fast, like she's been running.

"Don't you come near me!" she hisses in a loud whisper. She brandishes the chair—one of those rounded plastic ones with metal legs. Orange. Cracked seat. He can't believe he's noticing the *chair* in such detail at this moment. The woman makes a weird, jerking motion—she jabs the chair at him, like you'd taunt a lion or a bull to charge. Phil wonders if the fat woman is a lion tamer—is that her job? The thought strikes him funny, and he almost laughs, and then he thinks, what am I laughing for? That's something a crazy person would do.

"Don't you come *near* me!" she whispers again—not really a whisper, but a kind of croak. "I know . . . types like you," she says. Desperate sounding. Gasping for air.

"Lady," Phil says, and shakes his head. He doesn't know what to say. He could tell her that she's fat and ugly, the last person on the face of the earth he'd want to get near, but it's probably not such a good idea.

"No," she says. He hasn't moved, but she shrinks away as though he'd just reached out and tried to touch her. "You shut up. Don't you talk. Don't you move. Don't you come near me!"

The druggie is still staring into his dryer. Big help. It figures that the only person in this place who might come to his aid is some useless drughead who doesn't have any brain cells left, who doesn't even know what's going on. The hippie's not that far away from Phil, but he looks fuzzy, out of focus.

All Phil can hear is the fat woman's ragged breathing. Like she's been running . . . or like she's been using all her strength to fight off somebody bigger and heavier. It's hard for Phil to breathe too. The stale moist air in here is starting to choke him.

Phil shakes his head to try to clear it, and the woman jabs the chair at him again. She gives a kind of growl.

Think. What to do. It's not like he's scared, Phil says to himself, it's just that he doesn't know what to do.

Phil raises both hands slowly, like a criminal surrendering. Maybe if he whispers. "Lady," he whispers. "You've got the wrong guy. I haven't done anything."

Her eyes dart around, and she licks her lips nervously. Is this a good sign or a bad one?

"If you come near me, I'll scream," she says in a low voice. Her eyes on him are pure hatred.

With all her strength, she hurls the chair straight at him. He ducks and runs. Just runs. He hears the chair land with a *thwack* and a cracking sound. She's broken the damn chair right in two.

He hears his washer shimmying, finishing up the spin cycle, as he races past it toward the door. Out the door.

Now he's outside. What to do? There are all his wet clothes—every piece of clothes he owns—trapped inside that Laundromat with an insane woman who wants to kill him. He has to do something. What if he has to go home and tell Zeke that he let some crazy ugly woman scare him out of a Laundromat? He can hear Zeke laughing.

It's cold out—so cold it's hard to breathe. A white, heavy cold. His jacket's inside there too, and Phil starts to shake in his T-shirt, though he can't tell whether he's shaking out of cold or fear. He clenches his teeth, locks his arms across his chest. "Knock it off," he tells himself out loud, and the shaking stops, or almost stops.

It's going to snow, all right. Zeke'll be chomping at the bit to get started for Colorado. If Phil knows Zeke, Zeke'll want to head out this very evening, not even stick around for the party. That's starting to sound pretty good. To hell with *Women in Love*. That fat woman's probably got hold of it now, anyway. She's probably ripping it to shreds, chewing up the pages and spitting them out, writing obscene graffiti on the Laundromat walls with his highlighter pen. What did he do to make her hate him so much?

He could call somebody. He could call the police—but that would make what's happened seem too real. Maybe he could call Zeke, make it sound like a joke. He could say, "Zeke, you'll never believe what's going on here. You gotta come down here. You can't miss it. This crazy old bat, you've got to see her." Phil looks around, but there's no phone booth outside, no way to call Zeke or anybody else.

He looks inside the window of the Laundromat. There's the fat woman, and *she's* talking on the phone, a wall phone inside the Laundromat that he hadn't noticed before.

He doesn't stop to think. He opens the Laundromat door and stands on the threshold. He hesitates. He's scared to go back in, but he has to hear. Who the hell is she talking to? Maybe she's calling one of those numbers off the bulletin board. "Roommate Wanted: Must be Fat, Ugly, and Crazy."

But she's not calling any number off a bulletin board. It's the police she's talking to. "Please hurry," she's saying into the phone. "The Laundromat on 18th and P. He attacked me, he tried to rob me." Great. Just great.

And this is the thing that, for the first time, really scares Phil. The woman looks calm, not crazy and hysterical like before—and as she talks into the mouthpiece she swivels around and her eyes lock with Phil's. Just for a second, then she turns back and speaks into the phone again. "He's still here—just loitering outside. If you hurry, you can catch him." Her voice—it sounds so...sane. She sounds scared, but holding herself together. If Phil were the cop on the other end of that phone line, he'd believe her.

Phil looks at her—a frozen, snapshot moment. Maybe she's not that fat. Maybe she's not all that ugly. Maybe that housedress she's wearing isn't that frumpy—it's got a design of tulips on it. He hadn't noticed that. Maybe, when the cop pulls up in front of the Laundromat and goes inside and sees her, he'll think she looks all right. An honest citizen reporting a crime. She probably doesn't look any worse than the cop's wife.

And what will the cop think of him? Standing outside in a sweaty T-shirt and dirty sneakers. Shivering in a T-shirt, outside, in weather cold enough to snow. Cop's going to think he's on drugs, probably. He can't stop shivering.

Phil backs out the door again. His first thought is to run, but he can't. If you run, you look guilty.

He sees something going past his left shoulder—or, he doesn't *see* so much as *feel*, the way you feel a cat slinking past you in the dark. It's that hippie. He gets a glimpse of the hippie's ponytail as the jerk slides by, Phil's one witness deserting him. The hippie's probably got a sixth sense for cops, probably knows just when to get out before trouble comes. Has the hippie left his dried clothes in the dryer? Phil wonders. Would there be a way of tracing him from his clothes? Though there's no way to know if the hippie would tell the truth. Maybe he's so out of it he'd say, "Sure, I saw that guy try to rob that poor lady—saw it with my own eyes."

So what Phil does is sit down. There's a bench outside, and he sits down on it like he's waiting for a taxi. And then the cops are there before he can think.

He can't believe they got there so fast. The car pulls up, lights flashing. At least no siren—that has to be a good sign. If they thought this was a real emergency, there'd be a siren, like in the movies. And Phil would run to his car and screech out of the parking lot—high-speed chase.

Two of them get out of the car, a gray-haired cop and one that looks even younger than Phil. They manage to look bored and curious at the same time, holding out faint hope that this call might turn out to be interesting for a change, though they don't expect it to be. He stands up to greet them, feeling like he's the host of some *Twilight Zone* Laundromat party, and they're the first guests.

When they ask, he gives them his name: "Philip Jensen." He says Philip instead of Phil. They ask his occupation. He says, "Student." They exchange looks. What does that mean? Maybe the cops hate students. They probably do. Probably sick of breaking up drunken parties, sick of answering calls from frat boys who've had tape players stolen out of their BMWs. On a cop's salary, you can't afford a BMW or a tape player. Phil can't expect them to waste a whole lot of sympathy, even though he's never had, and never will have, a BMW. Not in this lifetime.

He remembers how calm and sane the fat lady sounded on the phone, and he tries the same approach. "Look," he says to them, "you've got the wrong guy. This is all a big misunderstanding—" But the older cop holds up his hand for Phil to be quiet. Like well-trained sheep dogs, the two cops nudge Phil inside without laying a hand on him, and there doesn't seem much point in arguing.

"That's him," the fat woman says immediately. She points straight at Phil, like they're already in court—he's the defendant and she's on the witness stand swearing on her stack of Bibles. "He's the one. He tried to rob me. Then he threw that chair at me." She makes her statement—cool, calm, detailed. How he had come up to her, and first she thought he was going to ask her how the machine worked, or how much soap to use.

"Kids ask me questions like that all the time," she says. "They never seem to know how to do their own laundry." Her voice has just the right tone—amusement plus mild exasperation at the irresponsibility of young people today. She smiles a little, crinkles up the corners of her eyes in a harmless, grandmotherly way. The way the older cop nods as he takes notes, Phil can tell the cop is warming to her. And why not? Right this minute she looks like somebody Phil himself might have asked for help and advice. Phil almost nods, too, and then catches himself, horrified.

For one second he was on her side. The fact makes him almost hyperventilate. Like something's shifted. The planet on its axis. Or worse, his own heart. He can't trust his own heart to beat the same way.

"But then," she says, her voice dropping lower and shaking

now, just a little, "he told me he had a knife, and that he was going to use it on me if I didn't give up all my money to him. When I said I didn't have any money—just change for the laundry—he got mad. He threw that chair at me." All this time, she doesn't look at him.

"Have you got a knife?" the younger cop asks Phil. He doesn't sound very interested.

"*No,*" says Phil. He empties his pockets, shows them comb, wallet, keys. No knife. Both cops shrug, unimpressed.

"Look," Phil says. "Look at the evidence. *She* threw that chair at *me.*" He points to the broken plastic chair, lying there in two pieces. "She was standing there"—he points, trying to reenact it—"and I was standing here. I ducked, and the chair missed me. That's why it landed way over there."

He points to his washer—his huge load of wet laundry. Why would he have bothered to do a load of laundry if his whole purpose for being here was robbery? His voice is shrill, rising. He can hear how hysterical he sounds. The way the younger cop is watching him, Phil can tell the younger cop thinks he's a creep.

"Did you throw that chair at this man, ma'am, like he says?" the older cop asks the woman.

The fat woman doesn't say a word, she just shakes her head no. Her silence is powerful—it makes all Phil's talking and pleading sound desperate, guilty, pathetic. He should shut up, but he can't.

"Look," he says again. "Why would I rob her? Look at my car out there—it's practically a new car. A Sunfire." (Though he was late with last month's payment, hasn't made this one. What if they find that out? What if they already know, somehow?) "I don't need some crazy woman's money. Does she look like somebody you'd *rob*? And here—" He tries to walk over to the table where *Women in Love* is, but the younger cop restrains him, so he has to point. His finger's shaking. "There. See? I was *reading*, for God's sake. A book for a class."

All *that* does is make the younger cop curl his lip.

"I think we better take this all down to the station, talk things over there," the older cop says with a weary air.

"You're arresting me?" Phil says in a whisper. Nothing louder than a whisper will come out. The older cop sighs and looks annoyed.

"I'll be happy to arrest you if that's what you want, Mr."—he checks his notes—"Jensen. Things would be a lot simpler if you'd just come down to the station, of your own volition, without anybody arresting anybody." Cop sounds like something straight out of *Dragnet*. Great. Phil's just been transported into an old *Dragnet* rerun.

"What if somebody steals my clothes while I'm gone?" It's a stupid thing to say, he knows, but suddenly it seems to matter. All his clothes—everything he owns—left for some stranger to find. What if that stupid hippie strolls back in once the coast is clear and steals his clothes? He can't stand the thought of it.

"Nobody's going to steal your clothes," says the younger cop, as though Phil's clothes are disgusting in some way, as though nobody in their right mind would want to touch them.

The woman has barely said a word since making her statement. She looks so cool and sane. Even her hair looks clean. Before, Phil swears, it was greasy and matted down. And her forehead was all sweaty . . . now it's not. How has she transformed herself from crazy to sane, from hysterical to calm, from dirty to clean, so completely?

Phil is wondering if it's true that you're allowed one phone call when you're arrested—and if so, who the hell will he call? Not Zeke, for sure. If he knows Zeke, Zeke saw that white sky and took off for Colorado already, without even waiting for Phil.

And then, as all four of them are on their way out the Laundromat door to the squad car, the younger cop accidentally brushes against the woman. Clearly an accident—both Phil and the older cop see him stumble, brush against her by mistake.

The woman turns on the younger cop, eyes wild.

"What did you do?" she asks, first softly, then louder, her voice rising in pitch like she's practicing scales. "What did you just do? What did you just do to me?"

Her breathing changes. She starts panting like an animal.

"Don't you come near me!" she says. "I know you!" Her eyes on the young cop are full of hate. The sweat on her forehead glistens. There are sweat stains on the underarms of her tulip-print dress.

She clutches her purse against her chest, as though the younger cop has tried to snatch it. She's forgotten that it's *Phil* who's the enemy. She's forgotten who she's supposed to be able to trust.

Phil sees a look of alarm, quickly masked, pass over the younger cop's face—the cop flinches, draws back just for a second from the woman. Phil is glad. Jerk. Thinks he's so righteous. *Now* how does he feel? As the woman screams, Phil almost smiles, but stops himself. It would look crazy, to smile at a moment like this.

◆

In the end, the woman is dealt with quietly, as an embarrassment. The older cop gets her calmed down, finally, asks her if she needs a ride home, if she needs someone to stay with her while she finishes her laundry, if she has anyone to go to, anyone to call. Phil can't hear her answers—her tone is low, appropriately low now, trying to make amends, trying to reestablish her sanity, but it's too late.

The younger cop doesn't do a thing—stands around looking at his fingernails. After a while the older cop comes over, pulls Phil aside, apologizes, calls him "Mr. Jensen" several times. Suggests that it might not be a bad idea to get away from the Laundromat for a while, come back for his clothes after the woman has had time to, well, clear out.

No kidding, says Phil. Laughs a little, shakes his head—so does the cop. They're on the same wavelength now, the same team. Everything's back in order.

◆

He drives around—just drives. It doesn't snow, after all. All that threatening, that heavy white sky, and nothing's happened. He keeps wondering if he's hungry. He ought to be. He hasn't had anything to eat in hours besides the Hershey bars and the Coke. He'd been planning on stopping for a burger on the way home from the Laundromat. He is hungry, he decides. He just can't think of anything he wants to eat.

The easiest thing to believe, of course, is that she was crazy, that she just flipped out and he happened to be in the wrong place at the wrong time. That's bad enough—the thought that you can't protect yourself from madness. But what's worse is the possibility that something in *him*, in Phil himself, set her off. What could it have been? He remembers looking at himself in that bathroom mirror, just before it all happened. He was avoiding looking at himself in that mirror, he remembers—he just can't remember why.

Instead of Phil, why didn't the woman choose that hippie staring into his dryer? Why didn't she assume the hippie was staring at her mirrored reflection in the plate-glass circle of his dryer, plotting how he was going to cut her up?

Why Phil?

He drives by Godfather's. He drives by the Taco Bell where he and Zeke usually go after parties. He drives by The Steak House where his father takes him twice a year.

He never in his life was so scared of anybody. He's always been big enough not to be picked on by other kids. And as for parents, teachers . . . cops for that matter . . . he's always known how to give them what they want, how to do just enough to stay out of trouble. It's been so easy. When he goes running, he wears shoes heavy enough to kick at dogs who show the least sign of attacking. He's always felt safe.

It's dark by the time he returns to the Laundromat.

He walks in slowly, almost on tiptoe.

She's gone. Part of him wants to get out of there, get back in his car and go home and not look back, just leave all his wet clothes there in the washer. But they're *his*. His things.

Nobody else is in the Laundromat, this time of night. Everything is just as he left it. His washer, closed and still, is waiting for him. The two crumpled Hershey bar wrappers and the empty Coke can on the end table, alongside *Women in Love*, the yellow highlighter pen marking his place, wherever it was. The broken chair is lying there on the floor in two pieces.

He walks over to the bulletin board and reads the notices on the bulletin board, the same notices the woman in the housedress had been reading just before she followed him to the bathroom. What had she seen? An ad for *tai chi* lessons. A notice for a revival meeting two nights ago. Another out-of-date notice, this one for a garage sale on September 28—over two months ago. A plaintive notice about a lost cat, answering to the name "Honey."

Phil goes over to the change machine and begins feeding dollar bills into it—every dollar bill he has. He loads his damp clothes from the washer into the dryer and starts it up. He feeds plenty of quarters into the dryer. He wants his clothes to be really dry when they're done, dry and warm, the kind of warm you can put against your cheek. Always before, he's tried to save money and time—jammed his damp clothes back into the laundry bag without taking the time to fold them. Not now. He's going to take a lot of time. He settles in. He picks up *Women in Love* and starts in on it again, right from the beginning. He's not going to Colorado, or anywhere else. Out of the corner of his eye he can see the hippie's clothes still there, sitting in the dryer in a soggy lump. Maybe the hippie will come back. He probably will, eventually. He'll stroll in, walk right over to Phil, and say to him in a soft voice, "Have you been saved?"

Sandra Dee Ate Here

Do you suppose this was ever true? Earl swears it's true, though Sandra's visit would have been before his time, so how would he know for sure? Earl has owned the Sandra Dee Ate Here for only ten years.

What *is* true is that there are three framed pictures of Sandra Dee on the restaurant's knotty pine walls. The largest is on the wall above the cash register so it will catch your eye when you come in, and you'll say, hey, this will be a good place to eat, celebrities eat here. Sandra Dee ate here. Hey, whatever happened to her anyway? That's what everybody says, except for the teenagers, who've never heard of Sandra Dee and don't care.

In the photograph above the cash register, Sandra Dee is posing on the beach wearing a modest two-piece like they wore back then, not a bikini, but still you can see what a pretty figure she has. The picture is signed, "Love and Kisses, Sandra Dee." The other two are head-and-shoulders shots, and they say only, "Love, Sandra Dee." They are probably from the *Tammy's in Love* era, and Sandra is looking up and off into the distance, gazing at some out-of-the-frame handsome stranger, probably. She is so beautiful and her expression communicates such wistful longing, such shy passion, that the handsome stranger would have to be an idiot not to pick up on her feelings. Who is the handsome stranger, anyway? Can anyone remember who the leading men were in those Tammy movies? I can't. That was before my time too.

Before I came to work at Sandra Dee Ate Here, I used to get Bobby Darin—who married Sandra—mixed up with Eddie Fisher. But I don't think people remember much about Eddie Fisher besides the fact that he left Debbie Reynolds for Liz Taylor, whereas Bobby Darin had that great, unforgettable song, and that to my mind makes him a legend. I'm not talking about "Mack the Knife"—I know that's the one most people remember him for—I'm talking about "Somewhere Beyond the Sea." You know how some songs can put a catch in your throat, make you sad without knowing why? "Somewhere Beyond the Sea" is one of those, and when I sing it along with the restaurant's jukebox, I can almost believe that Sandra Dee *was* here. If she was, if she truly ate here even once, it would make my job and my life mean more. It would make this town mean more. I know that might sound silly, but it's the truth.

Because this town exists on the promise of something happening, something big like Sandra Dee, and it would be nice to think that, at least one time, it did.

Tourists think it's so beautiful here on the ocean—which it is—that they feel a tug of longing as they drive through on their way north to one of the bigger towns like Tillamook or Astoria. If the feeling is strong enough, they slow down and change their plans and pull into the Sailor's Rest Motel. Then they go down to Fitch's, the one-and-only market in town, to look for a festive bottle of champagne. They don't even complain when they have to settle for something cheap and sweet, the only kind of champagne Fitch's carries. Usually it's too cold and windy to go down on the beach, so they head back to their cabin and sit at their window and drink champagne and wait hopefully for a pretty sunset over the ocean, but nine times out of ten all they get is fog. Which only makes them more filled with longing, because they know—they're just sure—that if they only had the time to stay one more night, which they don't, they would see the red-and-gold sunset of their dreams.

And then, the next morning, on their way out of town, they come into Sandra Dee Ate Here, all high and sparkly-eyed on the smell of manzanita and pine, and the glimpse they got, looking out to sea, of what they're sure was a whale or a sea lion. They order a big breakfast and tell me how beautiful it is in this town by the ocean and how lucky I am to live here. And if they're enthusiastic enough, and if the smell of the ocean that morning is fresh and sharp enough, sometimes I believe them.

But the locals, the teenagers especially, have a different view of things. The teenagers are BORED, and they wander this town looking so dark and angry that I'm almost scared of them, with all the things you read these days about gangs and drugs and kids with nothing to lose, but their boredom seems to take all the energy out of them, and even though they might *think* mean and awful things, they don't have the gumption to act. Still, I'm glad they don't use Sandra Dee Ate Here for a hangout. They go to Burger King. They walk past the Sandra Dee like it was invisible.

I want to shake them sometimes, to say to them, if you hate it here so much why don't you just leave—but they act like they've got no choice in the matter of their lives, like the pull of the tides just won't let them escape.

So which view of this town is the true one—the tourists' or the teenagers'? I honestly couldn't tell you. But I can tell you that sometimes I look at Sally, the other waitress at the Sandra Dee, and feel a chill. Sally's in her mid-forties, I think, though she looks older. She comes in bone-tired even at the *start* of her shift, and when I put "Mack the Knife" on the jukebox to get her blood moving, she doesn't seem to hear. She's not heavy, but she's heavy-footed. She makes the floor shake when she walks—just trudges from one table to the next. She's lived here all her life, she told me. I bet she was one of those bored teenagers once.

"Did you ever think about leaving?" I want to say to her sometimes, but the look on her face when I get close to asking her a personal question stops me. That's all right. There's a whole boatload of personal questions I don't want anyone asking me.

I never expected to end up in a place like this myself...but then, maybe Sandra Dee never expected to find herself off the beaten track either.

Here's what I think happened. If it is true that Sandra Dee ate here, then what I think happened is that one day after finishing a movie—or maybe after a fight with Bobby (who may have been a great singer, but probably a not-so-great husband, which I can relate to)—she just got in her car and drove up that winding coast highway from Hollywood. Finally on the third day of driving—because it could take that long, driving by yourself—she wound up at this little nowhere town on the northern coast of Oregon, and she thought, I'll just stop here and order myself a big breakfast.

The sharp cold sea air would have made Sandra hungry, and probably she would have felt reckless and rebellious, off on her own like that, and wouldn't have thought twice about going off her diet. Bacon and eggs-over-easy and an order of the fried potatoes Sandra Dee Ate Here is famous for. A big glass of orange juice. Coffee.

Maybe she even stayed here overnight—maybe even in the

same cabin at the Sailor's Rest, where I live. There are no rumors to that effect, but who's to say? It's possible.

At Sandra Dee Ate Here, Earl keeps a coffee cup in the front glass cabinet along with the Juicy Fruit and Tic Tacs he sells, and he claims it is a memento of Sandra's visit. The very cup she drank from. See? he says, and points to the faint lipstick mark on the rim of the cup. And it's true that the lipstick smear is a soft rosy pink, just the kind of color Sandra would have worn back then in her Tammy days.

It's probably too much to hope for that Sandra stayed at the Sailor's Rest. Earl owns the Sailor's Rest as well as the Sandra Dee, and he could easily have kept a pillow behind the front desk and claimed it as the pillow Sandra Dee laid her head on the night she checked in. And he's never done it. Earl's honest, which is why—even though he has no way of knowing for sure—I believe him when he says that Sandra Dee really did eat here.

Earl is fiftyish, tall, and just about the skinniest man I've ever seen, and he wears his thinning hair in a ponytail. He got laid off from a lumber mill in eastern Oregon ten years ago, moved here, and bought the Sandra Dee for a song, because the owner, a man named Harold, was going broke; Harold was so grateful to Earl for taking the Sandra Dee off his hands that he threw in the motel next door, the Sailor's Rest, practically for free.

That's pretty much all I know about Earl. I don't ask him questions, and I'm thankful he hasn't asked me any. When I applied for the job, he asked if I had any waitressing experience, and I said no, and he asked what had brought me here, and I told him I'd just run away from a bad marriage and was looking for a new life, and all he did was nod and say, "Can you start on Monday?" Because I'm so grateful to Earl, I haven't pointed out the suspicion that's occurred to me more than once: if Sandra Dee did eat here, and if she gave those pictures of herself to the restaurant's former owner Harold, as he claimed she did, why aren't they signed, "*To Harold*, Love and Kisses, Sandra Dee"? Who's to say Harold didn't just send away for some generic "Love, Sandra" pictures from her fan club?

Earl's done all right with the Sandra Dee and the Sailor's Rest—which is to say that he hasn't gone completely stone cold broke the way Harold before him did. Earl's converting the Sailor's Rest from tourist cabins to apartments for the regulars who live here year-round. Earl rents a cabin to me and one to Sally. He says he'd rather have a steady clientele than charge high tourist rates in the summer and have the place go empty the rest of the year, but I think he's doing it as a favor to Sally and me. We don't make much money, and he can't afford to pay us what he'd like. So this is a kind of room-and-board situation. We get to eat our meals at the restaurant for free. Earl lives in one of the cabins too, the one right in between Sally's and mine, in fact.

My cabin is the one farthest out on the cliff, the one closest to the ocean. I get the best view, but the worst wind. My cabin shields Earl's and Sally's from the brunt of it. During the bad storms, the wind howls and rattles my windows—one of these days all the glass is going to break, I just know it. Earl says no, it hasn't broken in the ten years he's owned the place, why should it break now? But I know better. That glass is getting weaker and weaker, and if I stay here, one of these days it's going to shatter, and then there'll be nothing between me and the storm.

Who would have thought things would turn out this way—the three of us, Earl and Sally and me, living at the Sailor's Rest like some weird family or some even weirder threesome? Sally has a crush on Earl, that's clear. And Earl—I'm pretty sure—is beginning to have a crush on me. I can feel his eyes linger on me longer than they used to. I hope Sally hasn't noticed, but I think she has.

After the Sandra Dee closes down for the evening, Sally usually says to Earl, in a low voice that she thinks I can't hear, "Interested in stopping by for a nightcap? I've got some brandy at home." He begs off almost every time, so that you'd think she'd take the hint, but she keeps asking, and maybe because he's so polite and gentlemanly and doesn't want to hurt her feelings, he gives in and says yes once in a while, and that keeps her going. I don't even think Sally's got something romantic, or even sexual, in mind. I think all she wants is a good drinking buddy, somebody to talk to. And after all, that's probably as hard to find as a good lover or the perfect husband.

◆

Tonight's a slow night, a Tuesday, and after over an hour when not a single customer has come into Sandra Dee Ate Here, Earl says, "Might as well close up a little early."

I nod. I wipe down the counter while Sally does the tables. Then I spritz a little Windex on Sandra Dee's pictures; I've started doing that lately, last thing before we close up. I don't want her to look all dusty and grimy, neglected and old, something for the teenagers to make fun of when they come in, though they almost never do come in.

Earl's eyes are on me. "That's a nice thing to do," he says, and smiles. "That's really nice."

Sally's eyes are on me too. This is the time when the lights are about to be turned out for the night, the time when she turns to Earl and says, "What about a nightcap?" But tonight she doesn't say it. She just puts on her coat and says good night, her heavy footsteps shaking the floor as she heads to the door.

After Sally leaves, Earl turns off the lights like he always does.

123

But then he says to me, "Wait. Wait just a minute." He turns the jukebox on, sets it to play "Somewhere Beyond the Sea" over and over again automatically. He holds out his arms. *Somewhere beyond the clouds*, sings Bobby Darin, *somewhere beyond the stars*. It's dark in the restaurant, but the jukebox casts a circle of blue-white light on the floor, like moonlight. I move into Earl's arms, and we dance.

Happy we'll be beyond the sea, and never again I'll go sailing, sings Bobby Darin, that song I could listen to over and over again forever.

Earl smells like salty French fries, but that's all right; I probably do too. He's so skinny I can feel his bones, but he's a good dancer. He surprises me, how good he is, how light on his feet. I could give myself up to a man who can dance like that. His hand on my back is warm. He's going to ask me to go home with him; I can feel it coming. I don't yet know what I'll say. It would be so easy to say yes, no big decision at all, really—his cabin's right next to mine, so it would almost be like going home. And besides, there's a wind up, and Earl's cabin would feel safer than mine, the glass in his windows less likely to shatter.

Or maybe I'll say no, because of Sally. But somehow I know it wouldn't be the first time Earl's disappointed her like that.

Whatever I decide, I know nothing will be the same after tonight. With that wind up, I can just feel what kind of storm it's going to be—the kind of storm that will wear itself out sometime during the night. The wind will blow every speck of fog far out to sea, and tomorrow will dawn clear and bright, the kind of day tourists fall in love with, the air sharp with the smell of pine and manzanita.

I'll get up before dawn and pack my bags. Before I go, I'll stop by the Sandra Dee and put on a pot of coffee, the way I always do. I'll drink some, and then leave the cup unwashed on the counter, lipstick stains and all.

Oh, I know it won't be long before people will forget I was ever here. Earl will be the only one to remember. I'm not like Sandra Dee, I'm not famous and never was and never will be, and nobody but Earl will have any reason to remember my name, or to wonder whatever happened to me or where I've gone. Even though I ate here, I really did, just like she did.

David Morning

Her friends Cheryl and Bill were always trying to set her up with some "nice interesting guy" or other, and finally Diane got tired of making excuses and said yes to this one, though the idea of a blind date horrified her. At thirty-one, she was too old for it. Too old, and far too cynical.

The blind date's name was David something. Diane didn't catch his last name when they were introduced—she thought it was Morrow or Monroe or possibly Moore. Or maybe even Morning. She liked the sound of that: David Morning. Morning was a whimsical, original name—the kind of name that made you happy just to hear it. But of course his name was probably not Morning.

It turned out, when she questioned Cheryl closely after the date (which she should have done to begin with), that Cheryl and Bill didn't know David well at all, as they had led her to believe. They themselves weren't quite sure what his last name was.

"Monroe," said Cheryl decisively.

"No," said Bill. "I'm sure not. It's Moore. David Moore. As

in, 'More cheese, please.'" He laughed, and Cheryl shook her head indulgently, a familiar gesture that let Diane know that "More cheese, please," was a joke. Bill was fond of silly jokes, jokes that defied explanation, jokes that made no sense. Cheryl called Bill's sense of humor "abstract."

Cheryl and Bill had met David Moore or Monroe or Morning at a charity fund-raiser. He could have been a con artist or a jewel thief or worse for all they knew.

The four of them went out for dinner. A double date—a concept that, like the blind date, seemed to guarantee an awkward and unpleasant experience. But it went beautifully. For once Bill didn't send back his poached salmon with complaints of over- or undercooking. David ate with a good hearty appetite but without taking much notice of the food, which pleased Diane. The last man she'd gone out with had felt it necessary to conduct tedious chats with waiters over the merits of orange duck versus seared monkfish.

After dinner, they all went back to Cheryl and Bill's place to play Trivial Pursuit.

It was 1983, and Trivial Pursuit had recently come on the market. Cheryl and Bill were always the first to buy whatever was new. They managed to make Diane feel like the country hick perpetually behind the times, even though they themselves had moved to San Francisco just a year before she had, and from the Midwest, too. Diane liked David instantly because he had never heard of Trivial Pursuit, and he didn't seem to realize that this was something he ought to be ashamed of.

And that was why it was a doubly nice revenge that David and Diane, who had never played Trivial Pursuit in their lives, trounced Cheryl and Bill the very first game. When Diane gave the right answer, *Peter Pan*, to the question, "What play explains the beginning of fairies?", David beamed at her. "She's an excellent partner," he said to Cheryl and Bill. "A perfect partner." He smiled again at Diane. "We're in tune," he said. And it did seem so. The words "Peter Pan" had sprung into her head as though by magic.

David answered the next question, "What was Elvis Presley's middle name?" with the correct answer, "Aron." He was modest when everyone applauded, said he didn't know how Elvis Presley's middle name had found its way into his subconscious; he had no idea he possessed such a fact.

Peter Pan, Elvis Presley. There seemed to be a connection there, though Diane didn't know what it was and didn't want to get her hopes up. Luckily, Cheryl and Bill were gracious losers, and did not seem to mind at all that they lost the game, and the one after, and the one after that. They laughed at their mistakes— they were great laughers, Cheryl and Bill, all of their friends loved that about them, the fact that they had such a good time together, no matter what they were doing.

At the end of the third game, which Cheryl lost by failing to identify the capital of Norway (not that Diane herself remembered, but still she smiled a little smugly when Cheryl drew a blank), Diane looked at her watch and stared. It was two-fifteen *a.m.*! She had thought it was about ten-thirty. Diane never lost track of time so completely. She was always the first to leave a party, always the one to start yawning when everybody else was just getting rolling. Cheryl and Bill were the life of any party— they were always talking about how they'd gone out dancing till four in the morning. Yet here they were yawning, while she and David smiled at each other and felt as if they could keep going all night, forever.

At last, at a quarter to four—David and Diane had just won another game—Cheryl said apologetically, "I'm afraid I'm starting to fade." David leaped up, mortified (as Diane should have done, and normally *would* have done—what was wrong with her?). "I had no idea it was so late," he kept saying. "Truly. Just absolutely no idea. I'm so sorry." He didn't look sorry—not in his heart of hearts. He gazed at Diane, and she saw stars in his eyes. She was his perfect partner. And he was hers. They were each other's perfect partner.

It had been a magical evening. No one had gotten angry. No one had gloated. David said it was just bad luck that Cheryl and Bill had rolled all the trick questions like, "Who was the last ruler in the Egyptian dynasty of the Ptolemies?" Who would have guessed Cleopatra? "I certainly wouldn't have," said David gallantly.

Diane, as eager as David to make sure that Cheryl and Bill weren't upset about losing, said yes, it *was* funny how she and David had just plain lucked out with the easy questions—and the playful, intuitive ones, the ones that wouldn't embarrass you even if you *did* get them wrong. Who would expect anyone to know Elvis Presley's middle name? So you could say whatever happened to spring into your head. And it just so happened that more often than not, whatever answer happened to spring into David's or Diane's head was the right answer. "It was weird, wasn't it?" she said to David. "Very weird," he said, and smiled at her.

Then David, who did not drive, called a cab and volunteered in the most gentlemanly way to see Diane home. But Cheryl and Bill pressed her to stay the night with them, and she agreed. (She'd done this before, on occasions when she'd spent the evening at their house. Diane didn't drive, either, and it seemed less trouble all around for her to curl up on the sofa in their study than call a cab or impose on Bill or one of the guests to drive her home.) Tonight, when she thought about leaving the warm nest of Cheryl and Bill's domestic bliss, going out into the night air into a cab with David alone, she shivered suddenly, afraid the spell of that perfect evening would break if she stepped outside.

So the last glimpse she had of David that night was the tail of his brown overcoat as he ran lightly down Cheryl and Bill's front steps to his cab. Diane had a sudden premonition she would never see him again. And that was the moment when she asked Cheryl what David's last name was, and it turned out that Cheryl and Bill didn't exactly know.

Suppose there was no David Morning in the telephone book? Suppose there were hundreds of David Moores and Monroes and Morrows, and none of them was the right David? Suppose he disappeared forever?

After Cheryl and Bill had gone to bed, Diane went into their study and stood at the window. The view from their study window was a familiar one, but it looked new tonight. The house across the way was owned by an artist, and it had a wonderful trompe l'oeil painting of a bright pink bougainvillea twining up the side of the house, curling around an upstairs window. The bougainvillea vine was so lifelike that Diane might have mistaken it for a real one, had not she and Cheryl and Bill one Sunday afternoon watched the artist painting it. They had sat on the steps drinking gin fizzes—Bill's specialty—watching the artist working on a scaffold. Watching him was like watching a beautifully choreographed dance. They weren't even afraid when he stood on tiptoe on the scaffolding, reaching to put the finishing touches on the last pink flower—his touch was that sure. It was one of those city miracles, one of those things that only happened in San Francisco.

The bougainvillea vine seemed to glow especially bright tonight—from moonlight, or starlight, or maybe only streetlights. Diane sighed a sigh of pleasure, tinged with sadness, at the pure beauty of it. She looked up at the stars, and then out at the city lights, and imagined herself as Wendy, holding onto Peter Pan's hand, flying through the night. It was easy to imagine soaring over

Russian Hill and Coit Tower and out over the Golden Gate Bridge and then circling back again, flying over Cheryl and Bill's house and finally back in through the study window—first touching down at the artist neighbor's house, hovering like a hummingbird over his magic bougainvillea.

◆

The next morning Diane awoke early. She could never sleep past seven-thirty, no matter how late she'd been up. Because she knew Cheryl and Bill wouldn't stir for hours (they bragged about how late they slept in on weekends, just as they bragged about how late they stayed up at night), she made herself a cup of tea and tiptoed silently through the kitchen and living room and pretended the house was hers and that David, her own dear husband, her perfect partner, slept lightly in the bedroom, his chest rising and falling softly.

When she had finished her tea, she went back into the study and smoothed the sofa and plumped the pillows, trying as always to make it look like she'd never been there at all. She didn't want to be a burden to Cheryl and Bill.

Diane took one last glance out the study window, and as she looked across at the bougainvillea vine (didn't it look a little too bright to be real this morning, a little gaudy?), she remembered the end of the story about the artist on his scaffold that lovely Sunday afternoon.

Bill had been so impressed by the artist's work that when the artist climbed down off his scaffold for a cigarette break, Bill had walked over to introduce himself and tell the artist of his appreciation and admiration.

He had returned almost immediately, looking embarrassed and crestfallen. Apparently the artist had been quite rude to him.

"Surly," said Bill. "That's what he was." The artist had told Bill he didn't like it when people watched him work, that he very much wished Cheryl and Bill and Diane would go inside and leave him alone.

And so they had—it was getting late anyway, and a little chilly. Bill had been upset, and Cheryl had leapt to his defense ("How dare he be so rude to you! How thoroughly uncalled for!" she said, almost in tears). They tried to shrug it off—they went out for dinner and tried to pretend nothing had happened, but their happy Sunday afternoon mood was spoiled. It was too bad.

But afterward, Diane noticed, whenever the subject of the artist's trompe l'oeil came up, Bill and Cheryl told the story of how they'd sat on the steps and watched the artist paint it. They talked about how wonderful it was to see the flowers and leaves take shape before their eyes. There was never any mention of the man's rudeness.

The first time Diane heard them tell the story, she wondered if they had collaborated in this revisionist version, or if they both truly believed it and had forgotten that she'd been there too. It never occurred to her to contradict them, to say, "Wait, it wasn't like that." And after she'd heard them tell their version a few times, the whole experience began to grow fuzzy in her mind. Maybe she had imagined the other, bad part of the story, the unhappy ending.

That morning, as she so often did, Diane left an affectionate thank-you note on the kitchen table, let herself out the front door without waking Cheryl and Bill, and took the Number 38–Geary bus back to her own little apartment, where none of her neighbors had hand-painted trompe l'oeil pictures on the sides of their houses, where the only view out the bedroom window (she didn't have a study) was of her neighbor's clothesline. Usually the scene depressed her—the contrast between her home and Cheryl and

Bill's—but this morning, buoyed by the night's happiness and success, she looked out her window and reveled in the sight of her neighbor's huge underpants and balloon brassieres flapping in the sunlight. The neighbor's clothesline could be an art object in itself, Diane thought. *Real* art, honest art, not some phony painting done by some surly jerk for the sole purpose of playing tricks on people's eyes.

◆

Well, naturally, she should have left things at that. At the mysterious David Morning—con artist, jewel thief. The elusive and perfect David Morning. Her dream partner, gone forever. That's the way it should have ended, with a last glimpse of his brown overcoat as he ran lightly down the steps and into that cab. With a lovely memory, and a renewed appreciation for herself and for her own life.

His name was, of course, not David Morning. "This is David Moore," he said when he phoned her the following evening. As in "More cheese, please." He spoke in a hopeful, tentative voice, as though he were aware of the spell the previous evening had cast over them both and did not want to risk breaking it. He told her that a coworker at his accounting firm was having a party, and he wondered if she might like to go. Diane accepted, in a tone as hushed and hopeful as his own. She was relieved he didn't suggest another evening of Trivial Pursuit. That would have been tempting fate beyond all reason, to expect such a perfect evening to repeat itself.

The coworker's party was loud and obnoxious, and Diane began yawning by ten o'clock and David got a killer migraine. (He was prone to killer migraines, he told her on the cab ride home—had been since childhood.) The host and hostess got into an ugly

argument. It was one of those uncomfortable public spectacles—
the wife sniping at the husband and pretending she was just
teasing, that her barbs were all in fun. The husband retaliated by
knocking back one Scotch after another and glaring at his wife as
though he was fantasizing various slow methods of murdering
her. David and Diane left the party early, and Diane was in bed—
alone—before midnight.

She went out with David again, however. The party's horrible-
ness was not *his* fault, after all. There was another date—a movie
that neither of them liked. And then there was another date—dinner at some new place that had been highly recommended by a
coworker of Diane's but was so disappointing that even David,
who rarely paid attention to what he ate, was annoyed.

During the course of these dates, it was revealed that David's
migraines were only part of a whole series of minor health complaints. Diane, who couldn't remember the last time she'd had a
headache, wasn't very sympathetic—was, in fact, a little bored
by David's ailments. And she could tell that he was irritated, just
a bit, by her lack of interest in politics, a deficiency that had
somehow never revealed itself during the Trivial Pursuit evening.
David loved to discuss politics. Not just national politics, which
she might, with effort, have managed to keep up with—but local
politics. He could recite the names of all the members of the
Board of Supervisors. Diane felt that he had misrepresented himself, masqueraded as David Morning, a light and magic person
who knew Elvis's middle name—when he was really a person who
pondered landfill legislation and property tax bases.

Before long, their dates became filled with long silences and
furtive glances at watches. They did not formally "break up."
Diane, later, couldn't quite remember how it had all finally dis-
integrated—whether she had made one too many excuses when

David called to suggest dinner or a movie, or whether he had simply stopped calling due to his own lack of interest.

◆

Two years went by. Diane took driving lessons and bought herself a car. She thought this would give her more independence, and surprisingly, it did. Her learning to drive altered, subtly, the dynamics of her friendship with Cheryl and Bill. Because she could drive herself home from evenings at their house, it no longer made sense to curl up on their couch at night. The three of them still spent time together, but a certain intimacy was gone.

Furthermore, Diane became engaged to a man named Mike, a man she met by pure chance when his car and her car were both in the shop together. It was, therefore, a match that Cheryl and Bill could take no credit for.

Mike was a burly man who looked like a football player but was in reality a lover of wordplay, the kind of person who turned to the "On Language" column in the *Times* the very first thing on a Sunday morning. Mike was a restorer of antique furniture. He had his own shop in the Richmond District and had built up quite a reputation. When Cheryl and Bill learned what Mike did for a living, they were impressed. Cheryl and Bill were always impressed by people who had interesting and unusual jobs.

One evening Diane and Mike were invited to dinner at the home of another couple, a couple they were just getting to know, and as an after-dinner entertainment, Trivial Pursuit was suggested. Diane had a bad feeling about the idea, but she was shy about vetoing the game for fear of being labeled a party pooper, which she so often felt that she was. But it *was* a bad idea to play Trivial Pursuit. Mike was short with her. He sneered when she gave the answer "Tennessee Williams" instead of "Eugene O'Neill" to the question, "Who was the author of the play *Long Day's Journey into Night*?"

("I did not sneer," he said on the drive home afterward, but he had sneered.)

After that, Diane's feelings were so hurt that she let Mike answer all the questions from then on. Even if it was an easy one like "How many sides does an octagon have?" she'd clamp her lips shut. Mike—insensitive clod—did not even notice that she was angry, that she was not contributing to the game. She spent the evening twisting her engagement ring, and on the way home she burst into tears. She was driving, and her tears blurred her vision, and anyway she was so angry that she *wanted* to crash Mike into a telephone pole. Mike held onto the car door handle and kept telling her to slow down, to calm down. "I don't understand why you're so angry," he kept saying.

"Of course I'm angry," she said. "What do you think? You made me feel stupid just because I couldn't answer that question."

"What are you talking about? I didn't make you feel stupid."

"How the hell do you know how you made me feel?"

The argument went on in this vein all the way back to Mike's apartment. She dropped Mike off at his door, leaving the engine running as an unsubtle hint. (Usually she spent the night.) He got out of the car and neither of them said good night.

Diane drove home and put on a flannel nightgown and looked out her bedroom window at her neighbor's clothesline, empty now. She thought of David Morning, her perfect partner, who had not crossed her mind for a long time. How enchanted David Morning had been when she came up with "Peter Pan" as the answer to that fairy tale question! As though Diane were an elusive, fairylike creature herself. And it was true she had felt special that night, the answers to those fanciful questions leaping, spontaneously, into her mind.

Spontaneity—that was what was missing in her relationship with Mike, she decided. Mike was completely lacking in spontaneity. He thought too much, analyzed too much, admired his own intellect far too much. Who *cared* who wrote *Long Day's Journey into Night*? What mattered was the play itself, the experience. The experience! She hated Mike.

◆

The next day, sober and subdued, Diane and Mike made up and vowed never to play Trivial Pursuit, or any game that involved pretentious pseudo-intellectual one-upmanship, or possibly any game at all, again. In this way they headed off a foolish and disastrous breakup, and in a year's time they got married.

They moved across the bay to Berkeley, where the rents were cheaper and there was more sun. The city fog was a problem in Mike's furniture restoration business—the damp air warped the wood.

Meanwhile, Diane's friendship with Cheryl and Bill had dwindled even more. Mike was allergic to cigarette smoke and could not stand to be around Bill for any length of time. Even when Bill was not smoking, the smell of smoke clung to him, and just being in the same room with him made Mike shudder.

Also, at one of Cheryl and Bill's parties, Bill had introduced Mike to an entire roomful of people as a "furniture repairman," without explaining the exact and specialized nature of Mike's work, and Mike had been furious.

Diane had pulled Mike aside and tried to calm him. "I think he meant it as a joke," she said tentatively. "I don't think he meant to insult you. Bill's sense of humor is a little abstract sometimes."

"Bill's sense of humor is retarded," growled Mike. "The man's a moron."

"*Sshh*," said Diane, afraid that Cheryl, standing nearby, would hear. She didn't think Cheryl heard. She was almost sure Cheryl hadn't heard.

After that party, Mike announced that he was never going to have anything to do with Bill again. Not under any circumstances.

Which would have been a problem, except that Diane's friendship with Cheryl and Bill was all but over anyway, not only because Diane owned a car and knew how to drive it, but because she had Mike. She suspected that Cheryl and Bill had rather enjoyed their protective, semi-pitying role in her life. They didn't know what to do with her now that they couldn't look for men to set her up with, now that they couldn't feel sorry for her.

The few times the three of them did get together, for coffee or lunch, they spent most of the time talking about how busy they all were and what a shame it was that they never had time just to kick back and spend an evening together the way they used to. Cheryl blamed it on the traffic jams on the Bay Bridge. They were worse all the time, she said, not just during rush hour but even late at night. She couldn't believe how hard it was, anymore, just to *get* to Berkeley to visit Diane and Mike. She spoke as though Berkeley was some frozen hinterland, accessible only by dog sled. She made Diane feel that there was something wrong with her and Mike for moving to Berkeley in the first place.

Still, Diane thought of Cheryl and Bill as her friends. So she was astonished one morning when, sipping her coffee, she opened the paper and saw a "Dissolution of Marriage" notice for Cheryl and Bill.

Cheryl and Bill had seemed like the rare sort of couple who would be together forever, indestructible, wearing their marital bliss like his-and-hers bulletproof vests. But it wasn't just the fact of the divorce that astounded her, it was that such a thing could have happened without her knowledge. Why had Cheryl not told her?

When Diane thought further about it, though, she realized that Cheryl had never, even at the height of their friendship, come to her with bad news or unhappiness. Diane had always naively assumed that there *was* no unhappiness in Cheryl's life. Now she realized the causes of the divorce could have been brewing all along without Diane even noticing, so absorbed had she been in her own lonely and emotionally impoverished state, so envious of what she assumed was Cheryl and Bill's perfect, smug stability.

For all Diane knew, on that magical night so long ago when she and David Morning had played Trivial Pursuit with such delirious happiness, Cheryl had been glaring at Bill across the board, despising him, wondering how to get rid of him. Maybe they had argued in bed that night, in fierce hushed whispers so Diane wouldn't hear, blaming each other for every wrong answer. Maybe Bill had called Cheryl a fool for not knowing that Oslo was the capital of Norway. "A ten-year-old would know that," he might have said. Maybe Cheryl had retaliated with tears, and the announcement that she had never, even in the beginning, found Bill sexually attractive.

In her sunny kitchen, with the smell of fresh coffee filling the air and Mike sleeping innocently in the bedroom, Diane looked down once again at the divorce notice and felt sad and terribly guilty. She and David Morning had been as self-absorbed as new lovers who kiss passionately in public—on subways, in the supermarket, in front of children—oblivious of the embarrassment they cause others. They had been so delighted in their discovery that they were perfect partners, so selfish in their happiness. They should have let Cheryl and Bill win just one game, at least. What would it have hurt to let them win just one?

Her friendship with Cheryl and Bill had always depended on their happiness and her unhappiness—that was so clear to her now. They had felt sorry for her, and she had been grateful for their concern. But that night, she had been happy. She had been the winner, they the losers. Marriages and friendships were as fragile and intricate as the workings of a clock. If one part were knocked the slightest bit askew, the whole thing ceased to function.

◆

What Diane did not know was that the Trivial Pursuit night had nothing to do with Cheryl and Bill's divorce. Cheryl and Bill had played Trivial Pursuit, and other games, so many times, with so many different sets of friends, that this particular night had made almost no impression on Cheryl. Cheryl barely remembered David Whatever-his-name-was.

No, what had knocked things out of whack was another night—the night of the party in which Bill had introduced Mike as a furniture repairman. Cheryl had, indeed, overheard Mike tell Diane that Bill was a moron, that his sense of humor was retarded.

"Why, he's right," Cheryl had thought, a light switching on over her head the way it happens in cartoons. She had stood stock-still, thinking back over all those times when Bill made jokes about cows chewing their gum. His jokes were stupid. Stupid and sometimes mean. He was no eccentric genius; he was a dolt.

From that night on, Bill's jokes got on Cheryl's nerves. She no longer laughed, nor shook her head in that affectionate, indulgent way. The spell was broken. His very presence, even when he was not telling jokes, became unbearable.

It was not Diane who was responsible for the breakup of Cheryl and Bill's marriage, therefore. It was Mike.

Then again, if Diane had never met Mike, Bill would never

have introduced him as a furniture repairman. So maybe it *was* Diane's fault, after all.

But there was something even stranger than the fact that Cheryl did not remember the David Morning-Trivial Pursuit night. She also did not remember the Sunday afternoon unpleasantness with the artist and his trompe l'oeil bougainvillea.

In fact, though most of her memories involving Bill turned sour after the divorce, that one did not. Whenever she thought of that Sunday afternoon, Cheryl remembered it fondly. She remembered the artist (who had long since moved, leaving his work of art to fade) putting the final flourish on the topmost bougainvillea flower, straining on tiptoe. Cheryl remembered the two of them, herself and Bill (she had forgotten Diane was there too), cheering him on.

When he was finished, she remembered, she and Bill had applauded wildly, and the artist had smiled across at them and waved, and then had taken a funny exaggerated bow. It had been a glorious moment, an unexpected and perfect moment. In fact, Cheryl thought, it was too bad that she and Bill could not have shared more experiences like that—maybe then their marriage could have survived.

What had been so lovely, Cheryl remembered, was that it had been as if she and Bill had collaborated with the artist in the creation of his picture. They had sent him their energy and enthusiasm, and he had used it. Cheryl could close her eyes and see the moment, *experience* the moment, as if it were happening all over again—she and Bill applauding wildly, the artist doing that funny little bow. She could see the bougainvillea vine glowing so brightly in the sun, the tips of its leaves catching the light, looking real enough to fool anybody.

Soft Money

We have lots of it, suddenly. No hard but lots and lots of soft. So this year in lieu of raises we are getting our offices redone. Ergonomic chairs in our choice of mauve or gray. Brand-new file cabinets and computers, new desks in faux wood. We can have our offices repainted in an approved color. Rumor has it that if you are on the manager's favored list, you can even get the department to pay for new Levelor blinds (though an official memo has been put out denying this, so I don't know what to believe).

But here's the problem. I don't like mauve. I don't like new. I don't mean to complain; it seems ungracious. And I don't want to make waves, because with all this soft money floating around and no hard, it's ominous. You could find yourself fired in the time it takes the manager to snap his fingers. In the old days of hard money and no soft, before the word *ergonomic* had been heard of, I used to sing along with the radio on my way to work. (I would never get a car tape player because the radio surprises you. All of a sudden there's the Mamas and Papas singing "California Dreaming," and you think, oh, *that* song. I love that song. Hearing it again is an unexpected gift, the voice of an old friend you'd thought you'd lost.) Now I don't even turn on the radio. I spend the drive cataloging sins I might have committed. I put them in three categories: sins bad enough to get fired, sins not bad enough to get fired, sins maybe bad enough to get fired.

And here's what worries me: if you start to *feel* expendable, you might start *being* expendable. You start to wear an aura of expendability, like a cheap perfume.

But there's the other way of looking at it: if you're expendable, then you have nothing to lose.

I've never been one to decorate my office. Those personalized touches, the family-photo cubes and artificial flowers and racy birthday cards from one's spouse displayed prominently—those things have always looked a little pathetic to me, a way of saying, See? I *do* have a life. I do. I'm not just work. But most of us *are* just work, and what's the point of denying it?

But. The color I want my office painted is not on the approved list. The color I want is that deep blue you only get on long summer evenings, when the sunset lingers for hours and finally turns into an intense glowing blue, lit from behind.

Besides, the manager of our department has been acting magnanimous since the announcement of the redecoration project, as if all of this soft money is *his* money that he's donating out of the goodness of his heart. Who does he think he's kidding? He made up the list of approved colors. It will please me to turn down his phony largesse.

So this weekend I go in, and the first thing I do, just as a timid first step, is take out a little watercolor brush and paint my office doorknob gold, and everything follows from there.

I have the whole building to myself. Sometimes people work

on weekends, but this morning when I go in, the place has that hushed feeling that makes me feel fairly sure no one else is here.

I get out the big brush and go straight to work repainting my walls. When they turn that rich luminescent blue, everything changes, as I suspected it would.

I've brought a couple of Persian carpets from home, the ones I bought long ago at a rummage sale for ten dollars apiece because they were threadbare and falling apart. You can hold them up to the light and see through them. Their colors have faded to gray-violet, gray-pink, gray-blue.

I don't want a new faux-wood desk, or any desk. I own a wrought-iron four-poster bed, and I see no reason not to have it in my office. My job involves a lot of reading, and writing reports on what I've read, and I like to read in bed.

Easy chairs, I've brought those too. A mouse lives in one—that dusty-rose one with the stuffing leaking out.

My office is a corner office, and to this day, I can't believe my luck in getting it. I put in for it three years ago, after Daniel Molar retired and took his nameplate down from the door. I don't have enough seniority to deserve a corner office, much less one this size. My coworkers, I know, think I must have bribed or blackmailed the manager to get it. That's what Mort Hasslebaum is always insinuating, every time he passes by and sticks his head in my door, but it's not true. All I did was put in a request for it, and it turned out that I was the only one who did. Why shouldn't it have been given to me, since no one else wanted it? Mort Hasslebaum has forgotten this, of course, but at the time he wouldn't have accepted this spacious corner office if it had been offered to him.

What happened was this: Daniel Molar was a bitter and solitary man who worked in this office for thirty years and ground his teeth with hatred every moment of his career. People thought "bad karma" and avoided Daniel. They went out of their way to avoid walking past his office. So no one really *looked* at it, you see. They probably assumed it was tiny and nondescript, possibly windowless, the kind of closet-next-to-the-elevator that you'd give to an unimportant guest at an overpriced and snobbish hotel. But I used to stop by Daniel Molar's office once in a while to share a pack of cinnamon candies with him and talk about swimming, his only passion. (And oh, I do like to think of Daniel Molar retired, just swimming and swimming, happy now for the first time in thirty years.)

Now that everyone sees how large and sunny Daniel Molar's office is and always was, they are jealous of me. But is it my fault I saw the possibilities in it where no one else did?

My office (whether I deserve it or not) is large and L-shaped. The L is so long, in fact, that you can't see the end of it if you just stand in the doorway. You have to be willing to come in a little way, and then you will have a treat. Then you will see the morning sun streaming in and making the dust motes dance.

There's a window at the end of the L that gets the very best of the early light. This morning, along with my glowing blue paint and the wrought-iron bed, I have brought some herbs and flowers in a cardboard box. I've decided to plant a window garden. Fennel and tansy to attract ladybugs and praying mantises, rue and pennyroyal to repel the department manager and Mort Hasslebaum. Pansies for luck, lavender for serenity.

As soon as I plant them, I can tell the flowers and herbs are going to love it here. You know how sometimes when you plant something, you just know immediately if it's going to thrive or not?

Encouraged, I put in a small reflection pool with goldfish. Not koi, because that would be pretentious. Just plain old garden-variety goldfish, two for a dollar.

Around the pool, I plant meadow grass, the kind with clover and wildflowers so I will hardly ever have to mow. The kind that attracts fat bumblebees, so zoned out on honey and pollen that it would never occur to them to sting.

Finally, I have brought a cat to work. He is black and white, oddly striped—a feline zebra. He is gentle, elderly enough to have sown his oats, content now to sit in the window garden and think back fondly over his wild youth. He is entertained by the sight of the goldfish swimming around, but too lazy to try to catch one. When he stares at his reflection in the goldfish pond, he seems to be contemplating the secrets of the universe.

I am just putting the finishing touches on my redecoration when Chuck, from down the hall, walks in. I hadn't heard him, and I give a little start. "Sorry," he says, and points to his stocking feet, which allowed him to enter without my hearing him. "More comfortable without shoes," he says, and I certainly understand that. We have a dress code, of course, but when you come in on weekends, you can allow yourself small liberties. Then Chuck sees my office, and gives a soft whistle. "Wow," he says.

Chuck is the sort of person who is serious, who always comes in on weekends to catch up. Even with all that hard money disappearing before our eyes, I'm positive Chuck will never be fired. *He* doesn't drive to work tallying up a mental list of his real and imaginary infractions. I'll bet he drives to work singing arias all the way. Chuck has a beautiful voice. I don't think most people have even noticed that about him. I like Chuck. He works on weekends, true, but that's no crime. (Better than Mort Hasslebaum, who claims to spend his weekends working, but who has ever seen him? Mort Hasslebaum is the kind of man who always, without fail, says "busy" when you ask him how he is.)

What happens next surprises me, because I would have thought

Chuck was happy in his office (which is even larger than mine and newly decorated in muted mauve), and probably he was one of the favored ones with access to the secret Levelor-blind slush fund . . . but Chuck takes one look at my office and says, "Can we trade?" That's even before he steps in far enough to see the garden and the cat (who looks up then, and blinks his gold eyes at Chuck, slowly, something he does only with people he likes).

"Why, of course," I say, without giving the matter a second thought. That may seem surprising, after all the work I've just done. But it's only a matter of painting the doorknob gold, and everything follows from there.

It turns out that I have made the right decision, because after I have begun to redecorate Chuck's old office—my new office—I discover a waterfall behind the door. We have a mandatory open-door policy—if our door is shut, the manager suspects we're in there doing something we're not supposed to do—so unless you closed the door you'd never even realize the waterfall was there. I wonder if Chuck himself ever noticed it? The waterfall gives off a lovely sparkling sound. I am going to like this new office.

Once I have finished redecorating Chuck's old office—my new office—I go down the hall and paint everybody's doorknobs gold, even Mort Hasslebaum's, and everything follows from there. I have plenty of luminous blue paint left—more, in fact, it seems, than when I started. And won't the manager be surprised when he comes in on Monday morning and sees what profound changes the soft money has made in all our lives?

The Salt of the Earth

On our third date, on the way home from the movie, Paul said, "Let's stop by my house for a minute. My mother wants to meet you."

That sounded ominous. But the minute I walked in the door, Paul's mother raced to hug me. "So this is Annie!" she cried. "I'm so happy you're here!"

I didn't know what to make of this. Nobody called me Annie; I hated the childish-sounding nickname, but when Paul's mother used it I didn't mind a bit. I was barely nineteen, desperate for approval, and accustomed to cool scrutiny by the parents of boys I went out with. "The last one was prettier, don't you think?" I imagined them saying to each other behind my back.

I was to learn that Rita—Paul's mother—would have rushed to embrace me if he had introduced me as an escaped convict. But I didn't know that then, and her eager, breathless affection was just what I needed. I surprised myself by throwing my arms around her and hugging her back.

"Come in!" she said. "Sit down. I've been watching a movie

on TV! What can I get you? Tea? Coffee? I sip coffee all night long, it seems like. I always have a pot going in case somebody drops in. Or Coke? Just whatever you'd like."

Rita wore black stretch pants, a bow blouse, and pink fuzzy slippers—frumpy clothes that had the shapeless mass-produced look of discount stores. But there was something innately stylish about her light quick gestures and fine-drawn features—an aura of faded-movie-star glamour.

I asked for a Coke, just to be polite. Paul requested ice water, and Rita rushed to fill our orders. Then we all sat in the dark living room. The television gave off a greenish tint. The only other light in the room came from a backward clock on the wall, the kind of novelty you sometimes see in bars, its backward numbers glowing yellow. There was a rocker and a Barcalounger, but instead of a normal sofa, two vinyl benches sat side-by-side against the wall. The benches looked odd there, as if they had come from a restaurant booth. I learned, later, that Paul's father was owner of the Dragonfly Bar and Grill, and that he was always hauling home items he thought the family could use: a bar stool covered in cracked green plastic, for example, that Rita had turned into a plant stand. He was especially proud of his idea to rip those benches out of a back booth nobody at the Dragonfly ever sat in anyway. Sofas were expensive; think of the money he'd saved.

But that night I knew none of this. I didn't know what Paul's father did for a living; I don't think Paul had even mentioned him.

"More Coke?" Rita cried suddenly, jumping up. My glass was full. I'd barely taken the first sip.

"Sit down, Mom," said Paul. "We're fine." He turned to me, smiling. "You can't come to our house without my mother jumping up and offering you things to eat and drink every five seconds. All she thinks about is feeding people."

Paul sat back, arms crossed over his chest, the picture of self-assurance. I envied that assurance; it was a quality I'd admired in Paul from the beginning. Yet in her eager desire to please I felt far more empathy with his mother. I smiled at her shyly, and she immediately smiled back. She was being so nice to me. And who was I? Just one more in a string of Paul's girlfriends. How could she even keep our names straight? Still, she had called me Annie, as though we'd been friends for years, kindred spirits.

Ominous music came from the television set, and Paul leaned toward it.

"I've been watching this old movie on television," Rita told us. "It's good. I don't know its name. I'm hopeless with names. It has Deborah Kerr, I think. And who's the man? Paul Newman, maybe."

"Charles Boyer, Mom," said Paul, smiling. "It's *Gaslight*, with Ingrid Bergman." He shook his head at me. "Deborah Kerr. And where did she get Paul Newman?"

"You see?" his mother said. She sounded absolutely delighted. "I told you I was hopeless. Paul's such a movie buff. He knows everything. I can't recognize anybody. I can't remember anybody's name."

We all turned to the screen. Ingrid Bergman stared up in wide-eyed terror at the ceiling; the gaslights dimmed and there came the sound of footsteps from the attic. That was it for Paul; he abandoned all attempts at conversation and sat forward, hypnotized by the movie. Rita appeared not to mind, or even to notice. She perched, birdlike, on the edge of the rocker and proceeded to tell me story after story of Paul's adorable childhood.

"...And there he was," said Rita, "two years old, standing on the kitchen counter pulling a butcher knife out of the knife rack. I never did figure out how he got up there. He stood there smiling at me like a little angel. I didn't have the heart to yell at him."

I gave Paul a sideways look. I'd have died if my mother had

started regaling a new boyfriend with embarrassing details from my childhood, but Paul seemed not to hear a word his mother was saying. He stared at the TV, even during the commercials.

"His baby sitter used to tell him he looked just like Tony Curtis," Rita said, leaning toward me confidingly in the dark. She lowered her voice. "I have to admit he was always my favorite child," she said, and added with unexpected immodesty, "He has my looks."

This was true. Paul and his mother were both slender and attractive, with dark brown eyes. When, later, I met Paul's younger brother Rod and his sister Debbie, they seemed like pale, washed-out versions of Paul. They "took after" their father, Rita said. But at that time, I didn't know what Paul's father looked like.

◆

"My old man drinks too much," Paul said to me a few nights later, his eyes on the waterbed commercial. We had just watched *Days of Wine and Roses* on late-night television, so I guess it was a good lead-in. We were at my house this time; my parents had already gone to bed.

"He had an accident a few years ago," Paul said. "Threw his back out in a major way. He's had a couple of operations since, but nothing's helped. So he drinks. He doesn't trust pain pills; he says they make him crazy."

"Oh," I said, casting around in my mind for the perfect, sensitive response that none of his previous girlfriends had been understanding or perceptive enough to think of.

But maybe I didn't have to say anything. Paul didn't look upset. He might have been discussing Jack Lemmon's acting career instead of his own father's drinking problem. He shrugged. "He spends most evenings at the Dragonfly Bar. He owns the place, so he hangs around there pretending to work. So. In case you're wondering why you haven't met him, that's why."

◆

Paul's father was named Marv. That, and the fact that he owned the Dragonfly Bar and Grill and that he drank, was all I knew about him for weeks, maybe months. He took shape in my mind as a silhouette—a shadowy, faceless presence.

Occasionally, when Paul and I went over to Paul's house to talk to Rita or eat one of her meals, we'd hear a truck pulling into the gravel driveway. Rita would listen and say, "There's Marv," and we'd fall silent in mid-gesture, a spoon halfway to a mouth, a hand reaching out for a water glass.

Sometimes there would be no further sound. That meant Paul's father had pulled into the garage and simply stayed there, passing out in his pickup truck. Other times there would be the slam of the screen door and footsteps trudging up the back stairs; that meant Paul's father wasn't quite so drunk and was able to navigate the stairs to his own bed. Either way, Rita would say, "I wonder if I should keep his dinner warm. Maybe he'll want to eat when he wakes up. I'll save some just in case." Then she'd smile and say, "But now, you two go ahead and eat. What will you have with dinner, Annie? Some coffee, some wine, both? Paul? What can I get you?"

Rita's cooking was like nothing I'd ever come across in my life. She had her specialties. She'd say, "Come over on Sunday. I'm going to make my tacos," or "my flank steak and fried potatoes," or "my macaroni salad."

The fried potatoes swam in butter and grease; the macaroni in the salad had been boiled until it had begun to disintegrate and then bathed in quantities of Miracle Whip, which Paul's father brought home in gallon jars from the restaurant. In Rita's kitchen were restaurant-sized containers of everything: giant jars of ketchup, a lifetime bottle of Tabasco. She used all these ingredients liberally. She was a generous cook—generous with spices, generous with the time she spent in the kitchen. Her cooking was Mom's Home Cooking with a vengeance.

It didn't occur to me to criticize it, though, not even inwardly. I was dopily, desperately in love with Paul by that time. I was nineteen. I wouldn't have dreamed of questioning a single thing about him. That vacant, slack-jawed stare that came over him when he listened to music or watched television only indicated a depth of concentration and an intensity of spirit. His mother's spaghetti sauce with its secret ingredients of pickle relish and Worcestershire was wonderful; whatever problems I had swallowing it lay in my bland and unadventurous palate.

And as for his father's drinking problem, what drinking problem? I had never seen it.

◆

One Saturday night, Paul and Rita and I were sitting down to a meal of Rita's navy bean soup and fried bread when there came the noise of wheels on gravel. We all stopped short, and then I put my spoon down. This was a new set of wheels.

Marv, drunk, always pulled into the driveway in a slow, deliberate way, proving to some imaginary policeman that he wasn't drunk at all, look how carefully he was driving. But now the gravel was flying; a car, something lighter than a pickup, screeched up and halted. A minute later the back door burst open, and two men and a woman stood there, smiling. I didn't know which of the men was Marv. I searched their faces for signs of resemblance to Paul and found none.

The woman was fiftyish and big-boned—not fat, exactly, but on the verge. She dressed in a way similar to the way Rita dressed, stretch pants and a polyester blouse, but she had none of Rita's natural elegance. Her makeup was thick and heavy, and her blond hair had the ratty look of too many perms and too many dye jobs.

"Hi, honey," she shouted, and threw her arms around Rita. I half expected Rita to draw back, but she didn't; she embraced the woman with equal enthusiasm. "Faye!" she cried.

"These men were a teensy bit drunk, and I didn't think I ought to let Marv drive, the condition he's in, so I brought everybody around in my car. I knew it, I knew it, I *told* Marv we'd be showing up right in the middle of your dinner. You must feel just exactly like shooting us. You go on and eat. Now that we've got Marv home safe and sound, we'll be on our way."

"You most certainly will not. There's plenty of food. Pull up a chair." Rita sounded thrilled to have unexpected guests showing up in the middle of dinner. And it was true there was plenty of food; she always cooked three times as much as she needed. "You too, Dale," said Rita to the big, ungainly man who stood next to Faye. "Sit right down."

So now I knew which man was which. Marv carried the party-sized bottle of Canadian whiskey he'd brought in with him to the center of the table. His walk was unsteady, and at first I thought he was reeling with drunkenness, but then I remembered what Paul had said about his back operations, and I realized that what he was doing was limping.

I had expected a monster, a dragon breathing fire and gin, but Marv was nothing like that. He was several inches shorter than Paul, and he was going a little bald and a little gray. He wore square dark-rimmed glasses, and looked as harmless as an accountant. He had a friendly manner and an easy, infectious laugh.

"So this is Paul's girlfriend," said Marv. "Hi, sweetie. It's nice to know you." I found I didn't mind being called "sweetie" any more than I minded being called Annie. *It's nice to know you.* It was a phrase I found enormously comforting—as though it were not only possible but easy to know another person that purely, that instantly.

Marv turned to Paul. "How's our boy?" he said with real tenderness, and reached over to touch Paul's shoulder.

Paul drew back—or rather, in. He stiffened, and said, "Great." I knew he was angry, but in a sudden shifting of alliances I sided with his father; Paul was being self-righteous. His father smiled across the table at me and gave a little wink. I smiled back.

Rita bustled to find extra bowls and silverware, and Faye, who seemed to know where everything was, rushed to help. Within seconds, the table was set and the food was passed just as if a dinner party for six had been planned all along.

"Well, we're celebrating," Faye announced, and lifted her glass. "Dale and I are getting married!" she practically shouted.

We all turned to Dale, who shifted, embarrassed. Like Faye, Dale was big and loose-fleshed. He looked like the kind of man who would be expansive and gregarious, but he wasn't. He stared down at his soup bowl and muttered, "We decided we might as well make it legal."

"You sneaky son of a bitch!" crowed Marv, slapping his thigh with delight. He reached across the table and punched Dale on the shoulder. "You didn't breathe a word of this. Why didn't you tell us?"

"We wanted it to be a surprise. We wanted to spring it on you," said Faye. "Guess we did, didn't we? Marv, I wish you could have seen your face!" She hooted with laughter.

Rita leaned over and hugged Faye. "I'm so happy for you, honey."

Faye brushed back tears. "Now look at me," she said. "Crying like a bride. Well, what the heck, that's what I am, isn't it?

It's just that you two are our best friends in the world, and I'm so happy you're here with us right now, you and Marv. You two are the salt of the earth. Hey, Dale!" she said suddenly. "Let's do this up right. Let's go to Vegas and take Marv and Rita along to be our best man and best lady. We'll drink champagne, play some blackjack, win enough to pay for the trip. What do you say?"

Dale shrugged. "Why the hell not?" he said. For some reason, this remark struck everyone as hilarious, and the table rocked with laughter.

After that, everything was funny. Any comment anybody made was greeted with whoops of laughter and Marv slapping his own knee if he couldn't reach anyone else's. He kept yelling at Dale, "You son of a bitch!" in the most delighted way. And even though the level of the bottle got lower and lower as the evening wore on, nobody seemed really drunk, just high-spirited. Even Rita took occasional birdlike sips from her own little glass of whiskey.

I wasn't drinking anything but Coke, but I began to feel lightheaded, lifted up by the party atmosphere. Even Paul seemed to be enjoying himself, not saying much but sitting back smiling in a daydreamy way.

Rita was in her element, leaping up and down, ladling extra helpings of bean soup. Her own food went untouched. As she passed plates and refilled glasses, she launched into a joke about two lawyers in a bar. "Or, no, wait, it was two doctors. That's right, it had to be doctors because one of them says to the other one, something about a stethoscope... No, wait, that's not right either." By the time Rita got to the punch line, which made no sense, even Dale was roaring with laughter.

"I swear she does this all the time," Marv said affectionately. "I never saw anybody get things so screwed up."

Rita shook her head and laughed. "It's true, it's true."

"That's so cute, honey," said Faye. "You are the cutest thing. You are our best friends in the world, you and Marv. You're going to be my best lady at my wedding, and I won't have it any other way."

And then things turned ugly. One minute everyone was laughing at a joke Faye had made on herself about wearing white on her wedding day, and the next minute Marv, reaching over to pat Faye on the thigh, said, "You old heifer! I can just picture you in white lace, all right!"

It might not have been so bad—one of those awkward moments, a joke that falls flat, an uncomfortable pause in which nobody quite knows what to say, and then somebody rushes to change the subject and the moment passes.

Rita tried. "More bread?" she said brightly, and passed the plate.

But then Marv, who hadn't noticed the lull, said it again. "You old heifer!" he shouted, and the word seemed to bounce around the room, echoing, and Marv kept laughing, the same laugh I'd found so charming and infectious earlier, only now it was going on too long and too loud. Even though I wasn't holding Paul's hand anymore, or touching him at all, I could feel his body stiffen beside me.

And Dale, who had been drinking straight shots of whiskey all evening, stood up clumsily, reeling, and slammed his fist on the table. Plates and glasses and silverware jumped, and I grabbed at my glass, but it was too late. Coke spilled everywhere and the glass rolled off and hit the floor. It didn't break, though; it was indestructible, restaurant-weight glass, courtesy of the Dragonfly Bar.

"You asshole, who are you calling a cow? That woman's going to be my wife, you sonofabitch!" roared Dale. He lumbered forward, lunging at Marv, then tripped over the glass on the floor. He almost went down, and clutched the table.

"Dale!" Faye tried to laugh, and the sound came out as a shrill hoot. "Come on, Dale! You know that's just Marv's way. Marv and I wouldn't know what to say to each other if we didn't insult each other. Come on now, you're being silly—"

Dale flailed like a parody of a drunk trying to fight. He jabbed at the air. Paul and Marv got on either side of him and held his arms, but Dale was strong. He pulled away, drew his elbow back, and hit Marv on the side of the face, open-handed, with a loud slap that echoed.

Marv staggered. For a moment I was afraid he was going to fall, but he held onto a chair and steadied himself. In slow motion, he raised his hand to his cheek. He didn't look angry, or even hurt, only confused. "Hey now," he said softly. "Hey now."

"You *idiot!*" Faye shouted. "Marv is your best friend in the world. Defending my honor, for God's sake. When I think of the names you've called me . . . Are you all right, Marv?"

"Sure," said Paul's father. "Sure." But then his face crumpled, and he grimaced and passed a hand over his face.

He was crying.

Rita sighed—a sound so soft I wasn't sure I even heard it.

Marv struggled to get himself under control. He lifted up his glasses and wiped away the tears. But his tears unleashed something in Dale, and now Dale began to cry, too—great howling sobs. He sank so heavily into his chair that I thought it would break.

"Oh, for Christ's sake," Faye said. "Well. Looks to me like we've worn out our welcome, doesn't it?" She turned to Rita. "I'm sorry, honey. These guys. I'd stay and help you clean up, but I think I'd better get this lunk home to bed. When they get like this, you know how it is."

"Isn't it the truth?" said Rita. She smiled. She even hugged Faye good-bye.

Paul and his father maneuvered Dale toward the door. Tears streamed down Dale's face. He clutched at Marv. "I'm sorry," Dale sobbed. "I'm sorry. You're my friend. Salt of the earth."

"You old sea horse," said Marv, his voice so brimming with emotion that he seemed on the verge of tears again. Fondly, he patted Dale on the shoulder.

I trailed after them. I stood in the doorway and watched them load Dale, like luggage, into the back seat of the car. Faye made her way to the driver's side, none too steadily. She saw me standing there and waved to me. Then she drove off, spraying gravel.

I went back inside and tried to help Rita clear the table. "No, no, no," she said. "I don't want you to do a thing." The empty whiskey bottle was nowhere in sight. She had already disposed of it, had already mopped up my spilled Coke.

I wanted to say something to comfort her. I looked at her fine tapered hands, the cheap white blouse with the ruffle around the neck, the delicate lines of her face.

Finally I said, "Maybe I should go, then. Maybe I should have Paul take me home."

"Oh, no, Annie! It's early. Stay and watch TV with me. It'll just take a minute to finish up these dishes." Her voice held almost the same tone of hearty hospitality she had used when Faye and Dale first showed up. If you didn't know, you wouldn't think anything bad had happened at all.

I went into the living room. Surely it had been no more than five minutes since Faye and Dale had driven away. Yet there was Marv, asleep in the Barcalounger as though he'd been there for hours. He might have been anybody's father, even my own, dozing after a home-cooked meal. The room was dark, but the television glowed; Paul had tuned in Johnny Carson. It was that late.

Paul lifted his eyebrows and gave me a brief smile. "Well," he said. "Now you've met my dad."

"Is he all right?"

"Just dandy," said Paul shortly. He turned back to the television.

I sat down on the edge of the restaurant-bench sofa. Rita came in with the coffee. Paul accepted a cup without taking his eyes off the screen. Rita poured a cup for me—I had begun drinking after-dinner coffee with her, because it was easier to accept it than to say "No, thank you," a dozen times in an evening. She sat down next to me.

The television glowed weirdly. There had always been something wrong with the color; Johnny and his guests looked lizard green.

"They're not even that good of friends, Faye and Dale," Rita said suddenly. "That's the funny thing. They're really not." And then she went on, as if it were all part of the same thought, "I almost married someone else." She leaned toward me in the dark. "No, I shouldn't put it like that. It never got to that point. Still, he proposed. He did. And I wanted to say yes."

She made no effort to lower her voice, but then, there didn't seem to be any reason to. Marv, there in the lounger, was dead asleep. The backward clock read twenty minutes after eleven. I had gotten so I could tell time by it as easily as I could by a normal clock.

"It was World War II," Rita said. "The day after Marv left to join the Army, his father came over with a letter from Marv. Folded up in the letter was an engagement ring. I was still in high school."

She glanced over at the sleeping Marv. Her gaze was deliberate, appraising. "I didn't want that ring. I can say that now. I couldn't, then, not even to myself. And anyway, how could I send it back, with him going off to war? Marv was so young, too. Barely twenty."

She held out her hand, looking at her wedding ring as though she couldn't for the life of her figure out how it got on her finger.

"I used to practice wearing that ring, at the Laundromat or a store where nobody knew me. I thought if I could just get used to the feel of it, I could get used to the thought of being married to Marvin. But I couldn't get used to it. And I got to thinking . . . who was to say I had to wear it? How would he know if I didn't? So I put it away, Annie. Just put it away." She sighed her barely audible sigh.

"Then I graduated and Marv was still at war, and I got a job in Santa Cruz working for Western Union. I loved that job. I loved Santa Cruz. It was a happy place, with the boardwalk, the roller coaster. You could almost forget that there was a war going on at all, except for all the servicemen around, on leave or in port for a night or two."

I could imagine just how it must have been. "I'll bet they all thought you were beautiful," I said. "Like Ann Blyth or Vivien Leigh. And one of them asked you to marry him."

She nodded. "Of course it was silly. We'd had two dates. Not even two. One-and-a-half. He had come into the Western Union office to send a telegram to his mother letting her know he was still safe, and when he was finished it was time for my coffee break, and he asked me to have coffee with him. That was our first date." She laughed. "Fifteen minutes long, to the minute. Western Union insisted on promptness. He made a joke of it, dragging out the seconds so he wouldn't have to take me back one second earlier than he had to."

There was a silence. It stretched on so long I finally realized the story was over.

Rita laughed, embarrassed. "Now you must never breathe a word, Annie. He's so jealous, Marv is. It was twenty-five years ago, but if he ever found out, it might as well have been yesterday."

Six feet away, in his Barcalounger, Marv snored lightly, even delicately. It wasn't an annoying sound at all; it was almost comforting. He still had his glasses on. I wondered whether tomorrow there would be a bruise where Dale had hit him.

"I guess it's better just to leave things the way they are, isn't it?" Rita said finally. "Not to think too much, or try to imagine your life turning out a different way."

Her eyes flickered to the television. Johnny or his guest must have said something funny; peals of laughter rippled from the studio audience. Paul never looked away from the screen.

Rita and I watched Johnny's mouth move, but if you had quizzed us, we wouldn't have been able to name any of Johnny's guests; we wouldn't have been able to retell a single one of Johnny's jokes without muffing the punch line.

I married Paul a year later, and six years after that we were divorced. In those years I ate many meals Rita had cooked, and I met a few more of Marv's true friends like Faye and Dale, hangers-on who showed up for the free liquor and food and never brought any of their own.

Slowly, the Dragonfly Bar went broke. Marv couldn't contain his peculiar habit of stealing from his own business. He supplied his family with food and furniture, his friends with liquor. An excess of generosity was his problem. He couldn't stop giving his friends drinks on the house, and then more drinks. It got to the point where he gave drinks away to strangers.

And then I left, and I don't know what finally happened to any of them, even Paul.

After the divorce, I replayed scenes from our life together. I still do. I try to uncover the moment when there might still have been the chance to turn things around. Sometimes I rewind even further, to our courtship, those first early days.

My memories focus more on Rita than Paul, though. When I left Paul, I ran for my own life, and abandoned Rita to hers. And even now, if I walked back into her living room right this minute, into that dark house, after all the bitterness between Paul and me and all those years, she'd throw her arms around me. "Annie!" she'd say. "It's so good to see you!" And she'd sit me down and make me drink a cup of coffee. The coffee would be bitter and muddy, but I'd drink it anyway. The pot would have been plugged in all day long, just on the chance that company would come.

Water Witch

Her older sisters are named Memoree, Melodee, Nola, and Twyla. Ellen doesn't know where her mother came up with these names, but whatever the imaginative source, it had dried up by the time Ellen came along.

Ellen's mother married Jim Reese straight out of high school and six months pregnant with Memoree. Melodee arrived a year and a half later, but then Ellen's mother decided she was tired of Jim Reese, and Nola and Twyla had a different father apiece. Ellen's mother never did bother with divorcing Jim, so when she decided it was time to have one last child, Jim Reese was who she went to.

Jim Reese doesn't have joint custody or anything formal like that—Ellen's mother still hasn't gotten around to divorcing him—but he lives in town, and if Ellen takes the roundabout way to and from school, she can pass right by the garage where he works. Sometimes she stops to talk; but usually he is busy or she is shy, and she just waves and goes on.

Jim Reese is the best auto mechanic in town. He can fix a car with a word or a touch. The way gypsies whisper horses, Jim Reese can make a car do anything he wants.

Jim Reese smiles a tentative smile whenever he sees Ellen walk by. The other sisters look and dress and even walk so much alike he can't tell them apart until they get close. And they don't usually get close. Memoree, Melodee, Twyla, and Nola walk on the other side of the street when they pass the garage. Sometimes Jim Reese sees boys drive by in cars, slowing down to talk to them or whistle at them. Boys in cars never slow down to look at Ellen, and Jim Reese can't understand this, though he is relieved by it. She is the prettiest one of all, he thinks, with her straight-as-a-stick blond hair and her round pale face. Ellen, his youngest, his baby.

◆

Ellen's mother's name is Pat. Her current boyfriend is a man named Pete, who sells carpeting and linoleum at Sears. Ellen's sisters think the sound of this is hysterical: Pete and Pat. Pat thinks so too. She's going to ditch Pete, she tells Melodee. She's going to dump him pretty soon. "He drinks Rolling Rock beer! In a bar he'll order me up a Rolling Rock without even asking for my preference. Plus, when we go out for coffee he slurps his in two gulps. No class. If we didn't ever go out, it might be all right. If we just stayed in bed all the time. But you can't do that."

"Why not?" asks Melodee. Melodee, who is twenty, has had affairs where you stayed in bed all the time.

"Well, you can do it for a while," says Pat.

One thing Pat has been doing since going out with Pete is buying higher and higher heeled shoes. Pete likes really high heels, pencil thin. He buys Pat the most expensive stockings he can find to go with the shoes.

"What a bore Pete is," says Memoree. "You should get rid of him."

"I know," says Pat with a sigh.

Pete has no idea Pat and her daughters are saying these things behind his back. Ellen feels a little sorry for Pete, but only a little.

◆

Ellen is fourteen years old, and her hobby is tending her garden. She's out in it now, at midday, a little apart from her sisters who are all sunbathing on the patio.

It's Friday, the twenty-third of June, and the July *Cosmopolitan*s have just arrived. Ellen's mother has taken out two subscriptions to *Cosmo*, but it isn't enough. The sisters squabble like children over it. They pull rank. Memoree is the oldest. She will be twenty-two her next birthday.

It's possible that none of them will ever leave. Melodee and Memoree occasionally disappear for days and nights at a time, when they're in the middle of a love affair, but they always show up again.

Memoree works part time at Fashion Delight, and Melodee works part time at Clothes Hut, and both of them spend their whole salaries on clothes. Pat doesn't mind; they buy clothes for her too with their employee discounts. The closets in the house are bursting.

◆

Ellen pulls weeds and imagines, the way she has done for as long as she can remember, that crickets and beetles and grasshoppers and ladybugs like to gather in her garden on hot afternoons and throw insect parties.

Under a white petunia, she sets a large flat stone—that is the insects' table. Around it she sets tiny smooth pebbles—these are the insects' chairs. She creases fresh mint leaves and sets them here and there on the grass in case the insects would like to use them for fragrant hammocks and nap in them after the party. She's bought a box of colored gravel—the kind you put in the bottom of a goldfish bowl if you have a goldfish—and has sprinkled the gravel all around the table to delight the insects' eyes.

Bees drift by, attracted by the coconut oil that Ellen's sisters have been massaging into their bodies. As they apply the oil, Ellen's sisters caress their own shoulders as tenderly as a lover would. All four sisters are lying out on Mexican blankets, drinking Diet Cherry Cokes, and fighting over the *Cosmo*s.

Ellen's sisters, and Pat, think Ellen has no experience whatsoever with sex. She's fourteen, and already they have written her off the way you write off a maiden aunt. It's true enough that Ellen has never actually had sex, but she thinks about it, and about love. Ellen once had her heart broken by a boy at school; it wasn't his fault. He had no idea she adored him; she'd never so much as said "hello" to him.

"Speaking of suicide," says Melodee. Her voice gets hushed. This is rare—Melodee usually talks so loud that at parties people tend to turn around and stare at her. Ellen has lost the thread of the conversation, but the word "suicide" makes her skin tingle, and she turns her ears toward Melodee like an alert deer. The other sisters wait expectantly. Melodee begins. "I was riding out in the country with Chuck last night."

"Oh?" says Memoree. "And what were you doing out in the country?"

"Wouldn't you like to know?" says Melodee, her voice a purr. "But anyway. We were driving under that overpass on Old Fort Road, and right across the top of it somebody had spray-painted the words, 'Lynn Come Back. Mike Needs You,' in silver glow-in-the-dark paint. They would've had to stand on the ledge of the overpass and lean over and spray-paint the words upside down, you know?"

"Lynn? And Mike?" says Memoree. "Do you mean—?"

"Sure," says Melodee. "Remember? Lynn was just telling us the other day that she'd broken up with Mike to go with Kenny Parks. So then"—and here Melodee's voice gets all soft and purring again—"afterward, Chuck and I were driving back into town, and when we got to the same overpass, there on the other side of it was *another* silver spray-painted sign that said, 'Lynn I Love You. Mike.' So I called Mike and asked him about it and he said, yeah, he and Jack and Ed got skunk drunk one night and went out and spray-painted the signs. He said if they don't work, he doesn't know what he's going to do. He said he feels like killing himself."

"So what did you do? Did you call Lynn?" asks Nola.

"Well, sure. And you know what? She hadn't even seen the signs. Pretty soon somebody will paint over them—the city or somebody. They might *already* have painted over them. She might never have known."

"So what's she going to do?"

"She doesn't know. She has to think about it. She really likes Kenny. But I told her, 'Mike says he feels like killing himself. Do you want that on your conscience?' So she's going to think about it."

"Mike's cute," says Twyla.

◆

Often when Ellen is close to the ground like this, tending her flowers, digging in the earth, she hears water rushing, as from an underground spring. She has a memory of herself as a child of five or six, camping with Pat and Jim Reese, while her older sisters went to their own summer camp. Ellen remembers this particular vacation very well. They drove for a long way until they came to a place by a stream. They rented their own log cabin, where they built fires in the fireplace at night, and Pat cooked trout that Jim Reese caught. The trout stream was so icy Ellen could hardly stand to wade in it; it brought tears to her eyes and took the feeling right out of her feet.

Union Creek, that was the name of this place out of Ellen's memory. Besides the creek, there was a pond with water lilies on it as big as dinner plates; and when they went walking in the woods, Ellen was almost afraid, because the forest was so dense and silent it seemed to close in around her like a cave. But in places, sunlight broke through. And even in the densest, darkest part of the forest, there were bright wildflowers.

When Ellen first brought it up, at the age of nine or ten, Pat said suspiciously, "I don't remember any such vacation—I think you're making it up. Why would I have gone on a trip with Jim Reese, that boring man? We weren't even living together then." But Ellen rattled off detail upon detail, and Pat was finally forced to say, "I guess it must have happened, then." She was amazed that Ellen, so tiny at the time, could remember such details. Pat doesn't like to think about the past at all; it evaporates behind her like mist on a hot morning.

So Ellen doesn't mention the trip again. But she thinks of that rushing creek water; the sound of it seems to be in her blood, something she is always hearing.

The dirt in this town is hard and dry and chalky. Ellen never realized it was problem dirt until one Sunday morning when she read an article in the gardening section of the local paper about the poverty of the soil—interviews with garden experts, tips on adding peat moss and bone meal. Ellen has never done any of these things. But everything grows for Ellen; she has a special touch. Maybe, she thinks, her garden is nourished by the underground stream she hears in her head.

It's four-thirty. Ellen loves the late afternoon sun and the lengthening shadows, and she stays outside in her garden. She nudges her favorite ladybug onto the end of her finger. She carries the ladybug over to one of her mint-leaf hammocks. To Ellen's delight, it stays on the hammock, as though pleased to be there. Ellen rocks the ladybug back and forth, so gently the leaf barely moves. She wonders if the ladybug appreciates the bits of colored gravel, glinting like diamonds in the sun.

The good tanning hours are over; the shadows are long on the grass; the ice in the Diet Cherry Cokes has melted. It's a Friday, and so, of course, the sisters all have upcoming dates. They go inside to bathe and dress and compare tans and change their nail polish. Then it will be time for Pat to come home from work, and Pat will go through the same ritual, except that instead of tight jeans she will put on stockings as delicate as mist, and a short, bright, flirty skirt, and she will sit in the living room with a Scotch-and-water, her legs crossed, and the four sisters, perfumed and tanned, will gather around her while they all wait for their dates to arrive—and they will talk about love and suicide, and when the timing might be right to ditch Pete.

◆

Jim Reese is finishing up his day at the garage. He explains to a lady in a blue dress why the engine of her Cutlass has been knocking. He doesn't really know why he takes the extra five or ten minutes to talk to customers like this—they have no interest in his work. Still, he wants her to know how carefully and diligently he has traced the source of the problem. This morning, almost in tears when she brought him the car, the woman had told him how frightened she'd been when it died suddenly in the middle of an intersection. So now, yes, she is grateful, but she isn't interested in details. She wants to believe only that it is fixed, once and for all, like magic.

Five o'clock on a Friday evening, and the town is gearing up. Teenage boys rev their engines, driving up and down Main Street, combing their hair in the rearview mirror. They have spent hours grooming their cars like horses—washing, currying, polishing, finally running their palms over shiny metal coats.

Now, his work day over, Jim Reese stands half in sun, half in the lengthening shadow of the garage awning.

Friday evenings are always hard for Jim Reese. He can, and usually does, clean up and then go down to the Rail Tavern to drink and shoot pool and talk to women and maybe even take one home, waking the next morning with the smell of her hair spray on his pillow. He usually enjoys the Rail Tavern once he gets there, but he never looks forward to it very much. The truth is, Jim Reese likes his work so much that when Friday evening comes around he doesn't want to go home. He fears losing his touch; he needs to feel the cold car parts, slick with grease, every day.

The early evening light has a metallic cast to it—the sun glowing like a bright copper penny—but the sky straight overhead is as blue as can be. Looking at the gathering procession of cars on Main Street, Jim Reese remembers the time when he was eighteen years old, driving down this same Main Street in a beat-up, used-to-be-silver Chevy Impala. Mouth dry, butterflies in his stomach, he was gearing up for a date with Pat Malloy.

Pat Malloy, who never, even at the innocent age of seventeen, was remotely starry-eyed over him. When Jim Reese said the words "I love you" to Pat, he said them from the depths of his naive eighteen-year-old soul. Pat assumed he said the words in order to get her into bed, and that was fine with her.

Jim Reese had always supposed that getting a girl pregnant

would be the worst thing in the world to do. He'd seen buddies of his break out in tears and cold sweats after losing this game of sexual Russian roulette. He'd always supposed that was the way he'd feel, too. But what happened instead, on the evening when Pat told him she was pregnant, was that he felt happier than he'd ever felt in his life. And when she said, calmly, that she wanted to get married, he hugged her close and hard. She let him, the way an impatient cat allows itself to be held, briefly, and then struggled out of his arms. She looked annoyed more than anything else. "What the hell," said Pat, "we knew we were taking a chance, right?"

The very next morning, Jim Reese had walked into Miller's Garage and asked the manager for a job working on cars. That was twenty-two years ago, and that manager has long since retired, and Jim Reese is still working at Miller's Garage. He is the one that people ask for, the one who can whisper cars the way gypsies whisper horses.

He knew from the beginning that Pat didn't love him, and he tried not to mind too much. He knew it wasn't anything personal. He knew if she'd married someone else, anyone else, it would have been the same. So he tried not to tear himself up over it, and when, after two years of living with him, Pat told him she wanted out, Jim Reese wasn't surprised. He moved out of the ramshackle house they'd bought, the house Pat still lives in, and into a tiny one-bedroom apartment over the Laundromat on Main Street, where he's been ever since.

He doesn't mind his little one-bedroom apartment—the heat from the washers and dryers rises and keeps him warm on cold nights. His heating bill is practically nothing. The only odd part of this arrangement is that he lives just a block away from the garage, and so he rarely has occasion to drive. His own car (another Impala, he has never been able to bring himself to buy anything else) sits unused, gathering dust, in a back corner of Miller's Garage. Almost the only driving Jim Reese does is when he test-drives his customers' cars to diagnose their problems.

There have been a few times over the years when Jim Reese has let himself dare to hope that Pat might someday come back to him. There was the time Ellen was conceived . . . and the handful of times since then when he's been in the Rail Tavern and Pat's come over and tapped him on the shoulder and asked him to dance a slow dance with her. After one of those times, when the music on the jukebox was especially slow and romantic, and Pat was in between boyfriends, Jim Reese screwed up his courage and asked Pat to bring Ellen and come camping with him at Union Creek for a week. When she said yes, he could hardly believe his ears. It's just as well he didn't let himself expect too much, because when the trip was over, Pat kissed him on the cheek and said, "That was fun," as though the whole glorious and idyllic week had been no more than a casual afternoon date to her. She gathered up five-year-old Ellen and went back to her own house and looked up an old boyfriend and started in again with him.

♦

On the sidewalk outside Melodee's friend Lynn's house, there is a message written in chalk rock, the same chalk rock you find in any backyard in this town, the same chalk that makes the soil so hard to work. The chalk rock message reads, "Come Back Lynn." When Lynn finds this message, she goes inside immediately to phone Melodee and ask advice.

Ellen lies down on the cooling grass and listens for the sound of an underground stream. Because it has happened before, it can happen again; Ellen knows all she has to do is be silent enough, listen closely enough. At that same moment, stepping out of

Miller's Garage, her father stands listening too, as though waiting for something to happen.

◆

Finally, Ellen wanders inside from the garden. The sisters have all left on their dates. "Will you be okay tonight, hon?" asks Pat, who is crunching the ice in her Scotch, waiting for Pete to come and pick her up. "Fix some macaroni and cheese. Make some of those new baby frozen peas. Do you want to invite somebody over to watch TV?"

"I might," says Ellen, who won't.

Then there is a honk. *Honk-honk-honk honnnnk*, goes Pete's horn. Pete likes to honk out little rhythms on his car horn.

"I can't *stand* that," says Pat, and grits her teeth. "I've told him and told him. When I leave him, he won't be able to say I didn't tell him." She gives Ellen a little wave and is gone.

Ellen thinks her mother is beautiful. Pat has the kind of body you see on ads for Special K. Ellen is not really fat, though she is fat by Melodee and Memoree's standards. Melodee and Memoree are always worriedly pinching the skin on their stomachs, checking to make sure they haven't gained. They live mainly on Diet Coke.

Ellen goes out back to her garden after Pat and Pete drive away. She wishes for a pretty rose-colored sunset, but the copper-penny sky has no pink in it.

They say a forked willow branch will lead you to water. They also say you don't even need the stick, that you can master the art of dowsing, water witching, by sense alone. Ellen read an article once about a modern-day woman who made her living doing it. Ellen likes the idea of this, leading farmers and builders to the right place to dig wells. She likes the idea of making a living by listening for underground streams in her mind.

The twilight air is dry as dust. Ellen thinks about water, why it is that there is dew on the grass in the early morning, even when it didn't rain the night before. Where does the water come from? How does it gather itself up in the night to form those droplets of dew? Early morning is her insects' favorite time. She imagines that her ladybug drinks dew from ivy leaves the way a cat laps milk from a saucer, delicately.

The party is over. The ladybug is the last guest of the afternoon, and it lifts itself off from the mint hammock and flies away home. After a moment's hesitation, Ellen gets up and follows in the direction where it went.

♦

Jim Reese doesn't really want to go to the Rail Tavern tonight. There is always the chance he'll see Pat there with a date, and the pain of seeing her is like a stomach cramp, sharp and debilitating.

He stands in front of the garage, reluctant to go inside and wash the car grease from his hands. After a while, in the distance, he sees Ellen approaching, her long hair pale as dandelion puff. She looks both ways twice, then crosses the street to him.

"Hi," she says. She never calls him by name—it seems disrespectful to call her father by his first name. Neither can she bring herself to call him Dad, because that implies an intimacy they've never had. Sometimes, in a whisper to herself, she says the words "my father."

"Hi, Ellen," says Jim Reese. "I saw your sister earlier. Nola I think it was. Drove by in a car with a boy."

"They're all out tonight. You'd probably see them all drive by if you stood here long enough."

There's a silence while Jim Reese studies the grease under his fingernails. "How's your mother?" he asks finally. He always asks this question, and it always seems to Ellen that it is painful for him to get the words out. "Will she be driving by too?"

"Probably."

"I see her sometimes. Driving by in a red Dodge Dart. That her boyfriend's car?"

"Pete," says Ellen, and Jim Reese smiles sadly.

"You want a Coke?" he asks her after a moment.

Miller's Garage has an ancient Coke machine, which has been kicked and dented in so many places it has a mottled texture all over. It's a temperamental machine, and Ellen has lost many quarters to it over the years, but Jim Reese never has. He knows just the right way to feed the quarters into the slot. He does it now, first rubbing the coins between his thumb and index finger for luck.

"A Coke is what you like, right? A just plain Coke? Not Cherry or Diet or anything, right?" He presents it to her as a gift, smiling his shy smile. He gets another for himself. They stand in the shade of the slanting garage roof. They watch the cars go by, cruising down Main Street.

"Does your mother like this new guy with the Dart? This Pete?"

"Not very much. He's on his way out, I think."

"Something's wrong with that Dart of his," Jim Reese says. "He revs it too hard at intersections. I've seen him do it. If he revs it like that in the mornings to start it up, he's going to ruin that car."

Ellen nods.

"You might mention that to him," says Jim.

♦

In the Rail Tavern, Pete and Pat are feeding quarters into the jukebox. Pat is feeling itchy. Pete goes to the bar and brings back two Rolling Rocks, and she glares at him. She spurns the Rolling Rock. She sidles up to the bar herself. She asks the bartender for a Scotch, double. "With crushed ice," she tells him, and she lingers on the *ssshh* of "crushed." Next to her, sitting at the bar, is Frank Flanagan, who dresses nattily and has worked as a clerk at the jewelry store for as long as Pat can remember. She and Jim Reese bought her wedding ring from him. Pat nods and smiles, the way she always does when she sees Frank at the Rail—but not quite the way she always does. Frank Flanagan sits up straighter, and when she reaches for her double Scotch, he says, "You sure got pretty hands. You could model rings, your hands are that pretty."

In the doorway of Miller's Garage, looking out onto the street, it feels to Ellen as if they are in a cave. The two or three cars parked in the darkness, left by customers to be worked on Monday morning, look like sleeping beasts. There is Jim Reese's own car, too, in a dusty corner. He walks back to it, takes out a handkerchief, dusts off the hood. "Go ahead," he says to Ellen, "sit down." She perches on the hood of the car, and he sits down beside her. "This is my car," he tells her, a little shyly, proudly. "Getting rusty. I should drive it more, give it some exercise."

She scrutinizes Jim Reese's old Impala. It looks old. It could be nine years old. It could be the very same car they took to Union Creek. She watches the dark sleeping car. Suddenly, she has never wanted anything so much in her life.

"Would you teach me to drive?" Ellen asks Jim Reese.

"Well, sure," says Jim Reese slowly. "I'd be pleased to. But you're not old enough. We should wait till you're old enough."

"Nobody'd have to know I'm not old enough, would they? Nobody'd have to know anything about it."

He shakes his head. "I don't know...."

There is a silence, and then she asks, "How old were you when you learned to drive?"

She feels him ponder this. She can barely breathe for the excitement.

He remembers driving his father's truck in a snowstorm when he was twelve years old; he remembers driving a tractor when he was even younger. After a long silence, he shrugs. "I guess I've been driving since I was born," he says.

Ellen claps her hands silently, the way she always does when she feels something wonderful is about to happen. She feels the way she felt when she was five years old, setting out with Jim Reese and Pat in the car on that camping trip to Union Creek, setting off on a journey to a new and secret place.

♦

Jim Reese drives them out onto one of the country roads west of town. When they get out far enough, Jim stops the car, and then he explains to her how to begin. How to work the stick shift, how to steer. He demonstrates reverse, first gear, second gear, third gear, back to second, back to first, as if he's moving in slow motion. She studies every move he makes.

"Now you try it," he says. "Try it real slow, real gentle."

Ellen slides behind the wheel. She tries out the feeling of her foot on the brake, presses down, lets up. She tries out the feel of the clutch. Then she sits for several minutes with the engine idling, putting all the movements together in her mind, like memorizing a dance.

She finally shifts into first, and they are off down the highway. When she shifts from first to second and then from second to third, she does it as easily and naturally as if she'd always known how. Jim Reese does not realize how unusual this is. He takes it for granted; he assumes everyone learns to drive this easily. He has never taught anyone to drive a stick shift. He doesn't even think of it as a skill to be learned.

Ellen shifts into fourth gear. They skim along, like some large low-flying bird. The road is easy, with gentle curves and hills.

"This is nice," says Jim Reese, and settles back. "Isn't this nice?" He isn't sleepy, only hypnotized by the lull of the road, and relaxed.

Then there is a change. The minutes go by, and they travel into that shadowy transitional time between dusk and darkness. Ellen leans forward and strains to readjust her vision. Only seconds ago she didn't need headlights; now, all of a sudden, she does. But she doesn't know how to turn them on.

"Look," she says to Jim Reese, "there's somebody in the middle of the road." She announces this calmly, until they get closer and it dawns on her that she doesn't know how to stop the car; she's forgotten that particular part of the lesson.

At sixty miles an hour, Ellen forgets what all the pedals mean. She slams her foot on the accelerator by mistake, and the car surges forward. Just in time she hits the brake, forgetting about the clutch entirely. The car screeches almost to a stop, lurches maniacally, and finally comes to a complete halt not six inches from the figure in the now-dark road, who stands still, its arms raised as though in surrender.

They all stay frozen like that. The scene is like a jigsaw puzzle that's been hurled into the air, and now they must wait for the pieces to come settling back down to earth and put themselves together.

Ellen looks down at her hands clutched on the steering wheel; they are cold with sweat, and slippery. Jim Reese's arms are out in front of him, hands braced against the dashboard.

Slowly, unsteadily, the figure in the road walks to Ellen's side of the car.

Ellen opens her window. She is sure the man—for it is a man, she realizes—will want to kill her for what she has done.

"I'm sorry," she tells him. Her voice won't rise above a whisper; the wind has been knocked out of her. "I didn't see you till the end. I didn't know how to stop the car. This was my first driving lesson."

"Jesus," says the man. He's younger than she'd thought, nineteen or twenty, and his face is pale beneath the beginning stubble of a beard. His voice, like Ellen's, is barely audible, and he clears his throat.

"Are you all right, son?" asks Jim Reese, leaning across Ellen and looking up at the boy.

"I'm okay, sir." The boy bends over to peer into the window and get a better look at Jim. "Just scared to death." He gives a funny, abrupt laugh.

More pieces of the jigsaw-puzzle scene fit themselves together in Ellen's mind. The boy's face is close to her now as he leans into the car window, and she realizes that at least part of what she had taken to be the pallor of fear on his face is instead a fine thin dusting of silver.

"What's your name?" says Jim Reese.

"Mike Carroll."

The silver is on his hands and his tanned arms, too, and on his faded jeans and red T-shirt. It gives him a moonlit, ghostly appearance.

So now Ellen knows not only who he is, she knows the reason for his suicide desire. She looks around for spray-painted signs of love. Sure enough, across the road in the middle of a rocky field is an old billboard. Who knows what the billboard used to say— the weathered letters of its advertised sign have been indecipherable for years. Mike has spray-painted over the letters with a single word: *Lynn. Lynn Lynn Lynn Lynn.* The name glows in the moonlight. Ellen turns away, looks straight ahead of her at the car's dashboard, so Mike won't know she's seen a thing.

Mike puts his hands on the car's window ledge, to steady himself. "It wasn't your fault," Mike tells Ellen. His voice is still shaky with fear. "I was standing out in the very middle of this road."

"It's more my fault than anybody's," says Jim Reese. "I wasn't paying attention. She was doing such a good job. I just settled back, forgot it was her first time behind the wheel."

"If you'd stopped the car the regular way, I wouldn't have been scared to death," says Mike. He leans a little closer, and says, as though telling her a secret, "I think it did me good."

"You better come along back with us," says Jim Reese.

Mike Carroll hesitates.

"Don't worry," says Ellen quickly. "I won't drive." This gets a laugh from Mike—a friendly, almost normal-sounding laugh. Then they both look at Jim Reese.

"Okay," he says. He gets out of the car and walks around to the driver's side. He gets in, glides his palms over the steering wheel.

Mike smiles. "I love these old Impalas." He walks to the passenger door, slides in beside Ellen. His face sparkles with silver, and there are dark shadows under his eyes. "Nice car," he says. "You could fix this up real special."

Jim Reese shrugs. "I fix up other people's cars."

Mike brightens. "You're the guy who works at Miller's, aren't you?" His voice hushes in admiration. Jim smiles modestly.

"He's my father," Ellen says, uttering these words aloud for the first time.

Jim puts the car in gear, and they start off down the highway, still heading west, away from town. The car falters a bit as they head up a hill. "It's acting a little rusty," Jim tells Mike.

Jim handles the car with a light touch, no macho posturing, no swaggering engine-revving. At the top of the hill, his hands hover above the steering wheel, so that for an instant the car seems to be driving itself.

"How far do you want to go?" Jim Reese asks Mike. "Are you in a hurry to get back?"

"No hurry," says Mike.

We could go as far as that line of trees against the horizon, Ellen thinks. That far, before we turn back.

"We'll keep going awhile, then," says Jim Reese.

Jim opens his window all the way, and Mike opens his, and Ellen lets the night fill up with sound: the hum of the car motor, the higher hum of crickets and grasshoppers. Beyond those sounds is the sound of an underground river, faint but unmistakable as the sound of blood rushing to the heart.

The Author

Helga Motley

Judith Slater grew up in Oregon and received her M.F.A. in creative writing from the University of Massachusetts at Amherst. Her stories have appeared in *Redbook, Seventeen, Greensboro Review, Sonora Review, American Literary Review, Beloit Fiction Journal,* and *Colorado Review,* among other magazines. She has twice received fellowships from the Nebraska Arts Council, and also two scholarships at the Bread Loaf Writers' Conference. In 1984 she was awarded the Henfield Foundation's Transatlantic Review Award in fiction. She is an associate professor of English at the University of Nebraska-Lincoln, and spends her summers in Ashland, Oregon.